TOBIE

TOBIE

A. Alex Come'

ARPress
45 Dan Road Suite 5
Canton MA 02021
Hotline: 1(888) 821-0229
Fax: 1(508) 545-7580

Ordering Information:
Quantity sales. Special discounts are available on quantity purchases by corporations, associations, and others. For details, contact the publisher at the address above.

Printed in the United States of America.

ISBN-13:   Softcover   979-8-89330-052-9
               eBook   979-8-89330-053-6

Library of Congress Control Number: 2024900794

Table of Contents

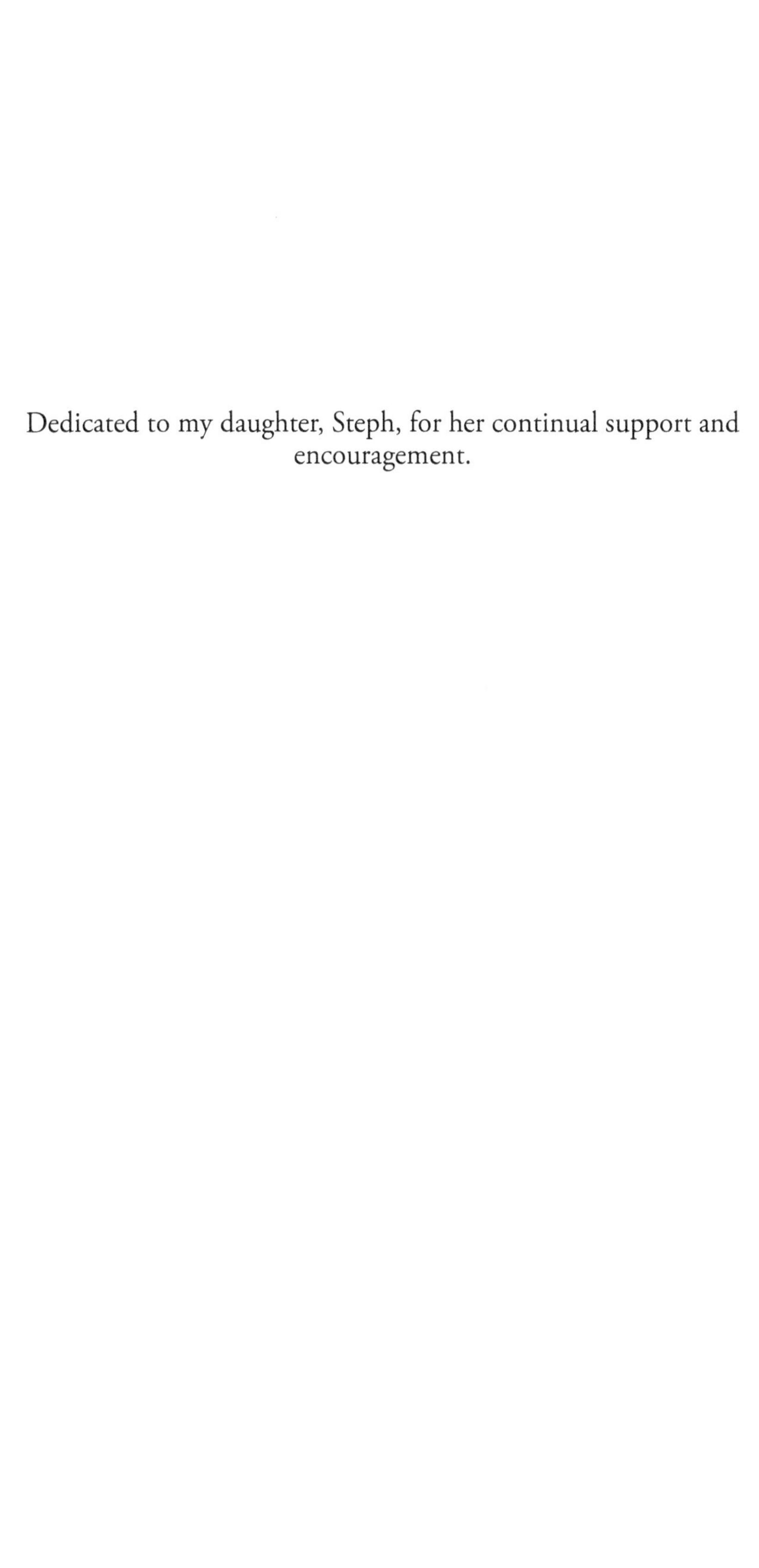

Dedicated to my daughter, Steph, for her continual support and
encouragement.

Chapter One

Winter, 1826
New Mexico Territory

The Indian woman had moved the two-month-old baby beneath her heavy Buffalo coat next to her body. The child had not cried even once because of the cold, and she was proud. He would, she decided, grow to be strong like his father.

Snow had been falling hard throughout the night, stopping only once just before dawn. It had made walking extremely difficult, and now she labored vigorously, working the snowshoes with quick, controlled steps. The wintery mountain air was thin, and thick ice covered the trees. But now a new snow was falling, and it would soon bury the tracks behind her. For that she was thankful, because the Apache war party was close, and relentless in their search. If caught, she would be raped then killed, and her son would be taken back to their village to be raised as one of them.

Stopping to catch her breath, she leaned against a huge spruce tree and closed her eyes. The freezing air caused a hard burning in her lungs, and her heart raced fiercely; she could feel it pounding in her temples. Having traveled through the night, her body ached and yearned for sleep, but there was no time. Loneliness and fear hounded her thinking, so evasively she envisioned her husband. He was a good man, loving and strong. And unlike the Indian male, he had always been gentle and affectionate, showing concern and valued her opinions. No better trapper or provider had she ever known. He was white but could have easily been a leader among her own people.

Forgetting the cold, she smiled as warm memories swam through her heart. She had liked the smell of his pipe tobacco. His smoking had been an evening ritual in their small Mountain Cabin and had come to represent a sense of security for her. For eternity, for as long as the stars of night shined their light, she would never forget his smile. For although he was tall, muscular, and brave, his smile always gave away the young boyish quality that had drawn her to him.

Wind howled and blew suddenly against the hood of her coat. Remembering where she was, she took a deep breath and continued her winter destiny, glancing back at the tracks behind her. Already they were disappearing.

The arrow seemed to fly out of nowhere, slicing through the thick coat and cutting deep into the flesh of her shoulder with agonizing pain. The impact knocked her backwards and she fell into the deep snow. Then came the cry of victory and he was on top of her with arrogance on his face. He was alone, and she wondered why as the steel blade of her knife stabbed into his neck with a sickening sound. Disbelief showed on his face as he fell across her body dead. Muffled cries came from beneath his heavy weight, and she quickly rolled him free of her.

Raising to a sitting position, she carefully checked the infant. Once satisfied he was okay, she laboriously rose to her feet. Pain shot through her shoulder, and for a few moments she rocked as she stood. Her head swam and she could feel warm blood running down her chest. She knew the cold would help stop the bleeding. Now she had but one chance: only one choice. If her baby were to survive, she must reach the foot of the mountain. Along the river to the white trading post; the very place she had met her husband. She and her father traveled there often to trade beaver furs and wool. That was where she had first seen him. So tall and handsome, filling the room with the pleasant smell of his pipe tobacco. He stood beside a crude wooden table, pretending not to be watching her. He was shy yet found the courage to approach her. Their eyes had met, and at that very moment, she knew the crossing of their paths had been predestined.

But that seemed so long ago. Several seasons have since passed. What could be said of their love; only that it had been wonderful? And out of it had come their precious son. She did not know now of her husband's predicament. Both she and the baby had fled their cabin, leaving him to face the attacking war party alone. She had wanted to stay, but it was not for her to decide. Perhaps he still lived; of this she did not know.

The weight of the snowshoes grew burdensome and heavy as she pushed on trough the mountain snow. Blood had stopped flowing from her shoulder, but the arm had grown numb and was now hanging worthlessly at her side. The pain was unbearable, and she fought unsuccessfully to put it out of her mind.

Snow was falling hard now; she could see little more than a foot in front of her. Yet on she struggled; her Pueblo blood running deep with determination, motivated by the small bundle of life beneath her cumbersome coat. Her feeble body was beginning to burn hot with fever, and she longed to shed the heavy fur. Sweat streaked her face despite the freezing air. To lie down would have felt wonderful. Refreshing. She wanted so badly to sleep. To just stop moving and rest. Her mind was clouding, growing distant from the reality around her; that could not be.

With a trembling hand she took hold of the arrow protruding from her shoulder. Following a deep breath, she jerked downward; a discreet scream left her throat echoing through the forest of endless trees. She staggered in the snow with incredible pain shooting through her body. It was a risky attempt to salvage her fading senses, and it worked. Slowly the pain subsided, and her head cleared. The bleeding would start again, she knew, but would not last long. With determination she continued her journey.

The blinding snow gave her little to go by in the determining direction. Her only clue was the sensation of a downward descent.

She longed for the day's past. For the feel of her husband's strong arms. For the security of their cabin, a warm fire, and the pleasant smell of pipe tobacco, of springtime and the beauty of flowers. And all the hopes of the future? She wanted so much to see her son grow, to mature into adulthood and give the precious gift of grandchildren.

Stumbling, she lost her balance and fell forward into the deep snow. Stabbing pain once again jolted her body; with effort she managed to roll onto her back. Concerned for the infant, she warmed her hand then checked his breathing. He had begun to cry but the moment she touched him, he quieted. Motionless, she lay staring up into the falling snowflakes. It felt wonderful to lie still and not move. Slowly her eyes closed.

The snow fell in a steady rhythm rapidly covering the dark Buffalo coat with white. Giant flakes, cool and refreshing, gathered on her face. Her breathing was slowing, the terrible cold was diminishing, and yet a radiant smile was showing on her face; for she stood in the heart of a beautiful meadow filled with flowers. A soft breeze blew, and a warm spring sun highlighted the splendid colors. A baby fawn bounced playfully before her in the waving grass. And high above in a sky rich with blue, a lone Eagle soared above calling out to her. Then she opened her eyes and screamed. Frozen, she tried to rise but could not.

Perhaps the Noble Bird had been sent by the Great Spirit to call out for help; she did not know. Suddenly, dressed in mountain furs and with a great white beard that virtually hid his face, the figure stepped quietly beside her frozen body looking down. Amidst the thick falling snow, she could barely see him. He appeared a giant, towering high above her. Then he kneeled, taking her hand. Only barely did she feel the touch. Yet with effort she grasped two of his fingers and ever so slowly moved his hand to the life beneath her coat. She mumbled words he could not hear above the wind, so lowering his head he placed an ear near her lips. She whispered only one word, and her life was over.

With difficulty, he opened the stiff coat and retrieved the tiny infant. He was very much alive and began to cry. 'Perhaps,' the trapper thought, 'he had begun crying over the death of his mother.'

Placing the baby beneath his own coat, he stood looking down on the dead woman. Seeing the arrow in her shoulder, he knew her journey had been a hard one. He had no idea who she was, perhaps one of the Dine people, a Navaho, or a Ute. Whoever she was, he admired her.

Turning, he walked away, descending the rest of the mountain to the warmth of the Trading Post below. Given the weather, it would be little more than a half hour walk. Thinking of the motherless baby now whimpering beneath his Coat, he sighed. South, in the town of Alburquerque, he knew of a Church, the San Felipe de Neri, it was told they would take in children with no home; and there was rumor of an orphanage being built. He would take the little being there.

When he reached the post, the snowfall had eased, and sunlight was now peeking through a clouded sky. Entering the thick wooden door, a dozen heads turned on him. Pulling the baby from beneath his coat he held him high saying with a smile, "Hey, my friends. Come and see what I have caught in my traps."

Laying the baby on the crude wooden table near the warm fire, he watched as the men gathered around. The infant looked up at him and smiled, kicking its feet, while waving both hands. The men laughed and talked among themselves sharing the joy of the tiny life. "What is the little man's name?" one asked. Glancing down at the little baby he said, "From the lips of his dying mother I heard but one word -Tobie".

CHAPTER TWO

Fall, 1834
Town of Alburquerque Orphanage

Wind crept down from the darkened hills like an invisible beast, howling at the tall adobe walls. Across the open desert, sand was blowing, and brush swayed; a cold gray sky held dim stars and thunder roared. Streaks of lightning flashed through the ghostly darkness and the promise of rain lay thick in the air. Hefty bodied, Widow Thachel, the Orphanage Overseer and mean as a Grizzley Bear and pack of wild Bore, would be sound asleep by now, and there was no better time to breakout.

Our bare feet felt cold against the rough wooden floor. Noiseless we sat on the edge of our beds staring at one another through the darkness; apprehension causing our heart to pound. The others were sleeping sound. Then, with a shrug, in unison, we rose and slipped quickly into our clothes.

As I dressed, my mind raced through the years I had spent here; from the moment I was old enough to start remembering, up to his very moment. Louie Henderson and I were best friends, and we had been through it all together: our first bottle of Whiskey and our first Cigar. The whiskey we had stolen off the wagon of an Elixir-Peddler claiming to be a Preacher doing work for the Maker, determined to help all who were sick, providing they had the money to afford feeling better.

But tonight, both of us, having turned the age of eight and going on nine, agreed we had grown enough to declare our self a man! Our minds were sure of it, and no one was about to tell us something different. It was time to be free, to do all the things we wanted. Time to be on our own and see all those exciting things out there just waiting for us.

Certainly, we would carry away memories, this place had been our entire life, our only family, a Children's Home yes, but the only place we had ever known. In both our minds there were two memories we knew we would forever carry; that old Elixir-Selling-Preacher who had provided Louie and me with our most cherished treasure to date; that full bottle of Whiskey and its sinful brother of pleasure, a great Cigar… or put truthfully, half-smoked, half chewed Cigar. He had tossed the old Stogie away while arriving at the Orphanage. We had watched it fly and splash down into a mudpuddle; but quickly snatched it up and hid it, anxiously waiting for it to dry in the warm summer sun; that treasure turned out to be the cat's meow; cat's meow was a saying Old Lady Thachel would use when good things turned her way favorably. And that is just how it turned out for us, the perfect smoke… except for the old Preacher's teeth marks, which we did not really mind. We figured the good Maker was looking down on us since even the old man's drooling, thick spittle, and yellowed teeth breath, had dried up in the blessed sunshine and vanished.

There would, however, remain one more memory I would hold on too, but never call it a fond remembrance; that being Ms. Thachel's Pet Cat; a humongous personally trained Feline Criminal – the dark love of Ms. Thachel's life, her mean, fat, Devil-Possessed behemoth she called…Tula Lee; who we called the Orphanage kid-hunter. The thing would hide in trees, rafters, around corners and in late evening wait in the shadows, just to jump one of the kids and scratch them till they screamed.

It was June early morning, the sun not up. At exactly 3:00 am Louie and I snuck outside to Thachel's bedroom window, and silently slid it open. Then, with what I thought was a firm grip, I held her evil Fur-Ball upside down while Louie saturated the Fat Cat's puckered-behind with Turpentine; an instantaneous cat resistance followed with claws slashing, my hands flying and regripping; it was a wild stream of meowing and hissing and me screaming in whispers; fat Tula Lee and me engaged in a right painful combat, until finally, with great determination and a lot of luck, I managed to toss the hairy monster through the window and on to sleeping Thachel's bed.

Louie and I made a run for it, back into the building, while behind us, there began a loud and wild onset of human screaming and Feline screeching; it was anoise- rage of great competition, just what we wanted. Things were toppling over and crashing to the hardwood floor, and amidst Thachel's yelling, came curse words… utterances so evil, even the Devil himself wouldn't blurt them out.

Back inside upstairs, Louie, I and half the kids scrambled to the window looking down at the noisy, Hell on Earth, open-windowed room of terror. We listened with laughter so loud it worried me the old lady might hear amid the screaming and screeching and flying fur! Then suddenly, we saw Tula Lee leap from the bedroom window with a screeching mad dash across the yard toward the river.

Old Lady Thachel's room fell silent, that was our que, quickly closing the window, we all scrambled to our beds, pulled up our covers and you would have thought a parcel of Angels were sound asleep dreaming about Heaven. Thachel came bounding up the stairway with Lantern held high. When she burst into the room, she discovered all her children in deep slumber. Beneath my blanket I thanked the Maker above, that none of the smaller kids giggled beneath their covers.

We had all made bets as to which female would scream the loudest. Louie and I knew we were going to get rich betting on old Fat Tula Lee.

However, after all our efforts, to quote Old Lady Thachel, there was no Cat's Meow for either one of us. We both went broke; I lost my only good pair of socks, a treasured pocketknife and a thick Feather Pillow sewed up only twice in four years. Who would have ever thought anyone could be louder than a big fat Cat with a Turpentined Pucker-Hole…and, adding to that injury; since I was the one holding Big Tula Lee when Louie poured on the Turpentine, that huge-clawed, kid-hating, fat fur of horror slashed me up right good. Tore me up so bad in fact, I feared I'd be scared for life.

And worse yet, when Old Lady Thachel connected my pitiful claw-streaked arms to her early morning distressful wakeup call; immediately I was pulled by the ear all the way to the woodshed; where, from the top of my tender butt cheeks, clear down my legs to the top of my feet, I became the Orphanages' welt-covered laughing-stock. For 24 hours, I had to parade around the grounds non-stop totally naked, with nothing to eat, nothing to drink and not allowed to speak to anyone. As if that weren't enough punishment and humiliation, in addition to my painful bewilderment, my best friend Louie had denied any involvement and got away Scott-free, every time he'd pass me by, he'd grin. And so it was, my best friend in the whole world, partner in crime, had walked away believed to be innocent by Ms. Thachel… except of course, late in that first afternoon, he happened to experience a fat lip and bloody nose!

Shaking away the memories, I refocused. The rain had begun; a light tapping on the dorm roof. Quiet as a couple of terrified rats, Louie and I made our way into the narrow hallway leading to the outside doorway. The interior adobe walls were rough on our hands as we felt our way through the cold stormy darkness. At the far end would be our long-awaited doorway to freedom, and the orphanage's history making, first great escape. Once in the yard, it would be over the wall and free. Although admittedly a little scared, there was no doubt in our manly minds that at the age of eight, we were ready for freedom.

As we approached the old lady's room, there was no guessing she was asleep; it was a well-known fact she could out-snore and out-fart any seasoned Cavalry Trooper, and this night was no exception, she was snoring and passing gas like dynamite exploding. And to our disliking, just as we passed her open doorway, lightning flashed silhouetting her huge sleeping shadow onto the wall right where we stood; thunder immediately followed bursting so loud we nearly filled our britches. Screams surged up our throats for escape, a terror cry that would wake the entire orphanage. Hands shot out to cover the mouth of the other, the way a man muzzles a horse. Frozen like that we stood motionless, mouths covered and waiting for Thachel to grab us by the scuff of our neck. But guardian Angels must have been with us, the old Lady didn't budge. For a few seconds we wondered if we should just forget it and turn back. Then lightning flashed again, and we caught a glimpse of the far doorway to freedom. Such a beautiful sight. With a nod, we started again.

The hallway was long and cold like an old ancient tunnel running on forever. My mind recalled a geography class Ms. Thachel had given on the country of Italy, about the city of Rome. She told of the miles and miles of dark tunnels far beneath the city, and how they were filled with bones and skeletons, hundreds of years of dead bodies. They had a name that I couldn't remember, something to do with a cat and a comb; I thought of fat Tula Lee and how Ms. Thachel would comb the cat's hair every night, then stuff the hair into her favorite pillow.

Rain had begun coming down harder now, a violent hammering. The air was growing colder, and the closer we came to the doorway, the colder it felt.

Then we were there! The moment of truth. Glancing back down the dark hallway we stood and waited, anticipating the next flash of lightning. One last lighted look back to ensure we were making the right decision. Then here it came; first the loud crash, followed by the split second of brilliant light, a clear vision. We wanted to scream! It was but a moment we saw her, hands on her hips and the look of death on her face.

We both yelled, knocking one another down, scrambling through the door to get out! Mud and water flew as we fell out into the soaked yard. I was the first to get to my feet. Again, lightning flashed, and I saw the ladder standing against the west wall, just where we knew it would be. Moving on a dead run I raced toward it with mud and water flying. The hard rain stung, but I didn't care; Old Lady Thachel was after me. I reached the ladder just before Louie, and in a heartbeat was up and on top yelling for him to hurry. He had made it halfway up when she grabbed him by the belt and kicked the ladder down. Soaking wet, shivering, and frightened, I stared down at them both. A flash of lightning illuminated the courtyard, and I saw their faces. Louie was crying and glaring up at me, but on the face of Old Lady Thachel… I saw the glimpse of a smile.

With a wet sleeve I wiped running water from my eyes, then shouted goodbye into the wind. I lowered myself over the far side and dropped. Climbing back to my feet I peered out into the cold darkness waiting for me. "Okay, Tobie." I told myself, "You're free. Now what?"

I hated leaving Louie like that, but what else was there to do? Maybe someday our paths will cross again.

That first night alone was terrifying. The rain didn't stop until shortly after sunup. I was cold and shivered through the long dark hours. There was no food, and I grew hungry. Midmorning Alburquerque was far behind me. The settlement sat in a large valley surrounded by mountains, and I took my last look down at it; by noon I was high and climbing. Whether someone would search for me I did not know. But if they did, I had no wish to be caught. If so, Ms. Thachel would not settle with the punishment of a welt-whipping, it would more likely be a hanging.

By the dark of the second night, I sat amid the rocks depressed, hungry, and lost. I would have given anything for food and water. The night air was freezing, and I shivered steadily. Fearful, I knew my strength was weakening and I thought I might die there alone.

As was always the case in New Mexico Territory, the night wind had come alive and began its antagonizing hounding. My shirttail whipped and hair blew wild. Looking into the sky and trembling worse than ever, I wondered if it might snow, it felt that cold. Few stars showed, and the moon hid itself beneath darkened clouds. The idea of ever feeling warmth again wasn't even imaginable. I stumbled frequently, out of strength. I was on my own now. No one to call out for help. It was up to me alone to make my way.

I wondered what kind of world I'd find if I didn't die. I had known nothing but the orphanage. Even my past was a mystery. I knew only that my mother was an Indian and that I had only one name, unlike the others. No one at the orphanage had known I came from Indian stock, except Ms. Thachel. No one could have guessed, since I did not look Indian except maybe for my black hair, and it was just as well since the Indians were feared and looked down on as little more than animals. But, to me, way down in a secret place within my heart, I was proud to have Indian blood. Ms. Thatchel had once told me my mother had been a brave and beautiful Indian woman; I knew she was dead, and of my father we knew nothing.

Often, while staring into a mirror, I would study my face - searching for the features of the Indian in me, but most of what I saw were those of a white boy. So, it became the strong belief my father was white. And at the age of eight, I was strong and a little taller than most of the others. If a fight came my way I would not run, but I did try to prevent it. I valued friendship yet considered my time alone to be just as important.

The orphanage behind me, the walking grew endless, the wind at night bitter, and my energy just continued to drain. I had no coat; shivering remained near violent, growing worse and worse; there was just no place to go for warmth.

Sometime just before daylight my strength and will to live gave out. Dropping to my knees shivering fiercely, I felt the world fading away. Toppling onto my left side, I heard the mountain wind howling like a call of death; and just before total nothingness came to swallow me, I told myself, 'Great decision, Tobie no last name, you ran away to be free…free to die!

Chapter Three

First Family

Death never came. When I awoke it was still dark, but I was no longer cold. Something heavy and warm covered me. Confused and disoriented, I lay quietly on my back trying to recall what had happened. I felt weak and my mind was sluggish, making it difficult to rationalize.

Slowly my eyes were adjusting. Then I saw the walls. They were circular. Fear stabbed my heart, and I sat straight up. 'Oh crap,' I whispered, 'the Indians have me, I'm in a Teepee'. Remembering the talk back at the orphanage, I knew I had to get out while I was still alive. In a panic, I threw back the heavy fur blanket and gasped. I WAS NAKED! 'Grap,' I thought, 'that was dirty. They'll take my hair next.'

Crawling on hands and knees, I moved to the covered exit, and picked up a small corner of hanging fur. Breathlessly, I peered out and a new kind of helpless washed over me, I wanted to cry. The Teepee stood in the middle of an entire Indian village. Indians were up and about everywhere, and it was broad daylight. There was no escape, I was doomed! Taking licks from Ms. Thachel's Razor Strap and Welt-Switch at the same time, would have looked more appealing than this. If I could have traded circumstances, I would have gladly dropped my britches and told Ms. Thachel to 'put it to me!'.

Then I saw him. He had to be the biggest man I'd ever seen; and he was heading my way. a Warrior Brave; probably the village executioner. Dropping the fur, I kneeled there by the exit. What to do?

My mind raced, and my heart pounded. The way I saw it, I had two choices: play dead or fight. I was too small to fight.

When he stooped to enter the teepee door, he found me lying motionless on the fur blanket face down of course. Leaving it open he hooked the fur door to the side. Now open, bright light poured in. Then he approached the area where I lay.

Kneeling at my side, he slowly rolled me onto my back and put an ear to my chest. I knew exactly what he was doing, and I held my breath with the greatest of skill. It was a game we had played often at the orphanage; a game I was a master at. But as is always the case, things seldom work out the way you plan. The lighted doorway darkened for a second, and I knew someone else had entered. Through a squinting eye I looked. It was a WOMAN! I made a face. Die or not,' I thought, I do have my dignity. Scrambling to a sitting position I pulled up my knees up tight, hiding my man stuff.

The pretending was over, I looked first at him then at her. Not a word was spoken. Silently, he rose and moved beside the woman. With sober faces they stood side by side, staring down at me, their faces were dimmed by the interior shadows, but I could see them. My heart lay in my throat. Somewhere outside, I heard a horse whiney and a muffled conversation. It was so quiet in my Teepee of Doom. I did not want to die, not yet, but I did expect the worst, and it happened. The Indian couple pulled their eyes from me and looked at one another, I knew it, they were ready to announce my fate. Heart pounding, my gut told me what they were about to say… 'we'll skin him first, then burn him at the stake'. But what came out of their mouth was worse, it was personal torture right there in the Teepee…the Indian couple holding my fate…suddenly burst hard into laughter, so loud the conversation outside stopped cold, the whole Indian Camp fell silent. And there I was, sitting helpless and naked on the Buffalo Blanket, my face red as the morning Sun, I figured out what it was they were laughing at - they were laughing at my man stuff, sure it was small, but surly they knew that given time, if they wouldn't kill me, it would grow up along with the rest of me!

To shorten a long story. That couple turned out to be incredibly special - the parents I never had. Through love and patience, they made me feel I belonged. There turned out to be six of us all together: Big Bear himself, Gentle Fawn his wife, two small daughters, and their own son, a year younger than myself. They called him Little Badger. He and I always went on hunting trips with Big Bear, and we loved it. He taught us to track and trap, to tan hides and make clothing, to appreciate all living things, and to survive using the same.

An old missionary many years before my time had taught Big Bear to speak English, and even how to read and write it. He in turn had taught it to his family. "A man's thirst for knowledge" he had once told me, "Should equal his thirst for food and water." Almost every night, we would take turns reading by the firelight from his favorite book, The White man's Bible. He especially liked the book of Psalms, probably because at times it told right and wrongs that often-paralleled Indian beliefs.

Big Bear was not a Christian man as one thinks in white man's terms. On the contrary, he upheld his Ute traditions with the greatest pride. He was just a compassionate being who, in his infinite wisdom, searched his entire earthly walk like so many others throughout history, in search for the secrets of life.

Many things I learned from that family, mostly the meaning of love, and the importance of life. Many memories were born and nourished in my heart during my time with them. Perhaps the most cherished took place in the spring of my first year. In appreciation for my growth in the Ute ways, Big Bear presented me with my own Indian Pony. He called the young filly 'Juanita' – named after a daughter they had lost during a terrible winter. I cried that day.

But things were not always a field of golden teepees, like the time Little Badger and I set out for the high country to become blood brothers. We figured that to be the best place to cut ourselves and mingle our blood, because there we would be close to the Great Spirit. We were on a half-day ride into the mountains when we felt the location was perfect.

We sat together, facing one another on a high ledge overlooking the green valley from which we had come. Far below, we could see tiny columns of smoke rising from camp cooking-fires and scattered rows of Teepees. The sky was immensely blue and filled with giant clouds of purest white. Birds sang their summer songs and never had I felt so close to my Indian brother and appreciative of my Indian Blood. Memories of the orphanage were far from me now, and I could not imagine a life away from my Ute family.

Badger drew his knife from its scabbard and a glitter of light flashed as the blade caught the sun. Proudly, but a little apprehensive, I gave him my left hand. Holding my index finger, he made a small slice along the bottom side as I squinted. Blood surfaced, and slowly rolled down into my palm. Then I drew my knife and took his finger. His face was strong and if he was scared at all, he did not show it. I had just started the cut when the thunderous roar of a Winchester Rifle echoed with frightening closeness. The bullet ricocheted off the rock between us, and we jerked, jumping straight to our feet.

The rifle was little more than twenty feet away. And holding it was the biggest, ugliest, smelliest man we'd ever seen. He was dressed in dirty buckskins, and his hair was greased back tightly to his head, probably held in place by animal fat. His teeth were rotted, and his nose was fat and large. While he waited for our hearts to stop pounding, he took time to laugh his foolish head off. He wasn't alone. Behind him stood three other men dressed almost the same way. There were also two women. They wore old dresses filled with holes and tears. On their heads were two of the silliest-looking hats ever made. The situation didn't look good for us. And when the leader quit laughing, things got worse. His voice was deep and harsh, like the sound of a file drug across metal.

"My name is Cannibal, and I hate Injuns."

Badger and I quickly looked at one another.

"You there, boy."

He was pointing directly at me, so I gave him my serious attention.

"You don't look like a redskin Injun to me."

I made no reply, he glanced back at the others behind him then and turned back to us; "Tell ya what I'm goanna do fer ya boys. I'm goanna give ya one of them multiple choices. Either I shoot ya where ya stand, ya jump off the cliff there behind ya, or ya take off all your clothes and do a rain dance fer us. It's been a mite dry in these parts lately."

The pack behind him laughed. Flustered, Badger and I looked at each other. We didn't say anything, there was no need. We really had no choice. Together we began removing our clothes. All the while we undressed the men never said one word, but those women couldn't stop giggling. I did not know about Little Badger, but as for me, I felt more like his brother than ever before, because at that moment, I was as red as he was.

Anyway. We did our part for the dry spell, whooping and howling like a couple of drunk Miners. It never did rain but when Cannibal yelled "git!", we got, racing away like wild wolves were after us. We must have been quite a sight, running north with our south sides flashing in the sun, and that wild group laughing themselves to death.

We had left our possessions behind, but at least we got away with our skin, even if it was bare. Besides, we could go back later and see if they left anything.

After a mile or so of running, we finally stopped and took time to catch our breath. Our heavy breathing was suddenly interrupted by Badger's excited voice.

"Great spirits of my ancestors," he said. "LOOK Tobie!"

I glanced over at him, and he was holding up his index finger, or at least what was left of it. The tip was missing. For a few silent seconds, we stared into one another's eyes with surprise on our faces. Then Badger smiled, and I followed suit.

"Well, my brother," he told me, "Next time it will be me who does all the cutting."

We burst into laughter and after touching our fingers, turned, and started back for our belongings.

Altogether. I spent nearly 8 years with those people. I learned a lot and cherished every minute. It was on a cold April morning that the Indian way of life I had known came to an end.

I had risen early that day. The Teepee fire had died, and it was still somewhat dark. Leaving the lodge, I walked toward the river gathering firewood. Three hundred yards from the village, I watched the first show of sun come up over the mountains. Then I heard the Bugles. They rang through the sleeping hills like the call of a wild animal - sending fear into my heart.

Dropping the wood I had gathered; I turned and ran for the camp. Young and healthy as I was, I just wasn't as fast as those cavalry ponies. They came thundering up behind me as if I were standing still. I never saw it coming but the sword came down across my chest with stunning impact. If the blade had not been pitched as it was, I would have been sliced deep to my heart. Still, the the blade that did catch me cut deep, and I felt warm blood pouring down my chest as I fell into the grass.

Fifty or sixty riders rode on past, down into the camp screaming and yelling like a bunch of wild animals. They were United States Cavalry, but you would never have guessed if it weren't for their uniforms. Some carried torches, and I cried every time they threw one on a teepee.

Bleeding and helpless, I laid in the grass watching. People I knew and loved ran from their homes, scared and screaming, only to be shot and trampled, or sliced with swords. I tried to rise but could not. I was losing a great deal of blood, and I knew I'd die if I did not stop it. With effort, I crawled to the river's edge and packed my wound with mud. Then falling back into the grass, I lay still. My head grew light, and everything around me dimmed. Far away, in what seemed like a vacuum, I heard screams and the horrible sound of repeated gunfire. The earth shook with the pounding of horse's hooves, and the smell of drifting smoke floated over the river. Then blackness came and I slept.

Sometime the next day, I awoke. I was too weak to stand, and for fear of re-opening my wound, I remained where I was. The day passed and night followed, bringing with it a starless sky. Except for a few berries, there was no food to give me strength. I drank plenty of water, and kept my wound plastered in mud. It was the afternoon of the second day that I dared chance standing. With the aid of an old limb, I slowly hobbled down to the camp, or what was left of it. Teepees lay in burned heaps, some still smoldering. Nearly everything was charred and black, including many of the bodies. Nothing moved, for nothing was left alive. Even pet dogs lay lifeless among the dead. The entire camp smelled of burned flesh and charred wood. The horses had run off into the hills, but I sensed Juanita would be somewhere nearby, if not killed or hauled away. She had become an inseparable companion over the years, and there was a special bond between us.

The village I had called home lay in a twisted, smoldering disarray. Except for the chirping of birds, I stood alone amid death and disbelief. The Teepee that had once been my home lay in a burned, distorted heap; nothing was left except three rib poles so charred they barely remained standing. In the middle of the wreckage were three bodies, naked and burned. The two girls would have been eleven and thirteen. Gentle Fawn lay in the middle. It was my guess she had died defending them. Which of the burned bodies that lay scattered about was Little Badger, I could not tell; tears filled my eyes, Badger was my brother of blood, we had grown together and close, inseparable and would have died fighting side by side.

It was on the western slope of the camp I found Big Bear. There at the tree line, eleven braves had been hung and he was one of them. Their lifeless bodies swayed gently in the afternoon breeze with the stretched ropes creaking with sadness. Once again tears welled.

After cutting him down, I closed his eyes and sat holding him in my arms. If he could have spoken to me, I know what he would have told me, "Let not your eyes cry, my son, but turn to the Great Spirit, and hear him say to you, 'There is only darkness in hatred, your true strength grows out of Love and Forgiveness".

But that day I did not want to forgive, I felt only hate. I vowed to remember. The rest of my life, I vowed to remember.

Chapter Four

1843

I was sixteen, and once again homeless. With the ability to read and write I would have an advantage over many. However, the only skill I possessed was knowing the ways of the Indian. All I had to do now was find a job requiring those abilities.

Big Bear and other men of the tribe had talked often of the scores of white people traveling west by Wagon Train. Perhaps, I thought, that would be the place for me since such adventures would require guidance and scouting. It had been rumored among the Ute people that such whites were crossing in hurds matching those of the great Buffalo.

I buried those I knew, then alone, left the ruins behind and headed east. With me were the only two possessions I owned; Juanita, my beloved pony and now the only living remnant of my Ute family, and Big Bear's prized Sharps Buffalo rifle which I called 'Old Bear,' in remembrance of him.

Independence, Missouri was a good 600 miles ride, but it was my goal. Scattered visitors to our village had spoken of this place being the starting point for many Wagon Trains heading West. Along the way I trapped and hunted, gathering furs to sell for money. And when I had acquired enough, and reached Independence, I shopped for the first time in a Mercantile. It was small and cramped but contained a great deal of different things. Shelves were stacked and prices were high.

What money I had went only so far. But I did purchase new clothes, a good saddle, a haircut, and a used handgun, a Navy Colt 44.

Luck turned out to be a good run for me. While in the barber chair watching eight years of hair and self-esteem fall to the floor, I noticed a waiting customer staring at me from time to time. Expecting trouble, I kept a loose hand near the forty-four. As I sat, I sized him up: a man in his late forties or early fifties wearing a gun but not strapped low, and the pistol was still held in place by the field strap. He was a short man, shorter than me, but stockier, however, a good thing was his face, it was easy, not the face of a trouble seeker. He wore his boots on the outside of his pants. which were Army blue and contained the yellow Officer 's stripe. His shirt was store-bought flannel and bright red, contrasting with his black suspenders.

As soon as the barber finished with me, I paid him and walked out onto the street walkway. The sun was bright and felt warm. Squinting, I pulled my new hat low over my eyes and stared out into the large street.

The stranger in the barber shop had followed me out and now stood to my right along the wooden walkway. Remaining silent he took out his makings and rolled out a cigarette, then lit it. The smoke smelled good as it drifted past.

People were everywhere. Unhitched wagons sat scattered in every direction, their tongues dropped into the hardened dirt as if in rest, while waiting for the hardships soon to befall them. Teamed wagons alive and noisy, clanged and clattered along the streets almost nonstop. Soldiers in uniform went about their daily business while women in bonnets chatted heartily, children played, and dogs barked. Then the man beside me spoke without looking at me. "I couldn't help notice you in the chair in there." He motioned with his thumb toward the barber shop and continued, "Don't mean any disrespect, but I was wondering if maybe you had Indian blood in you?" The question caught me off guard, and I didn't know whether to be angry or not. I took a minute to ponder the question, wondering why he would ask such a thing. Maybe my assumption about him was wrong. Perhaps he was hunting trouble; glancing down at his holster, the field strap was still in place. Looking back into the street I told him.

"I spent nearly four years in a Ute village with some of the finest people I've ever met. My mother was Indian my father white." My voice must have been edged with irritability for the man beside me replied defensively.

"Now hold on their young fellow. I don't mean to rile your pride. I'm just wondering if maybe you're looking for work."

For the first time, we turned and faced one another. His eyes were warm and spoke with kindness. Big Bear once said that the eyes of a man spoke truer words than his tongue.

He stuck out his hand and I took it.

"My name's Major Stumpp, retired, US Army". He smiled and I knew I'd like him.

"Tobie" I said as we let go. He continued.

"Right now, I'm a Wagon Master taking a train of folks across the trails and down into California. If you're interested, I could use another Scout. You're young." he said the words almost apologetically, then continued, "but I'm usually a good judge of character. Pays twenty dollars a month and all the beans and coffee you can tolerate. Of course, it won't be easy; it'll be a grueling trip, and long before we reach our destination a lot of folks will meet the elephant". He shrugged, looking straight into my eyes, "So, what do you say Mr. Tobie?"

Not wanting to appear as some overly anxious schoolboy, I stuck out my hand and gave a nod, "Well, Major, I'm your scout."

We talked for a while. He explained my job and all the dos and don'ts. I found out he had one other scout - the Master Scout, he called him. "He'd be a good man to learn from, Mr. Tobie". He told me. I figured as much myself, feeling eager to start.

We talked on, and all that time I was wondering, just what he had meant when he said a lot of the folks would meet the elephant. I never asked him, probably everyone in Independence knew and I in no way wanted to sound naive. Besides, I was pretty sure that long before our venture ended, I'd learn only too well.

Thirty-three wagons, single file beneath an early sky black and starry, left the town of Independence with a sense of excitement.

Within an hour, daylight would spill over the prairie ahead and chase away the morning chill. In my thoughts were visions of hardship, but also there harbored a bit of excitement of my own.

The master scout who I had met prior, answered to the name Steely. He was a quiet man and much a loner, but I felt comfortable around him and knew he liked me. Impressed with him, I knew he would be as I had thought, a good man to learn from. He was a skilled scout and had traveled extensively with Army survey teams exploring and mapping unknown territories. Though he did not mention it himself, it was said he had served with the Louis and Clark expedition of 1804. Although older than the Major, old Steely held him in high regard, not at all hesitant to address him as 'Sir' As it turned out, my being an inexperienced young man in this new life, it turned out a grand opportunity serving and learning under two such men.

The Nebraska flatlands began our long tedious passage. Farther west we traveled, terrain changes came, some good, even breathtaking, however, for the most part, the relentless hot sun glared with unyielding disconcert. It burned the skin and dehydrated our bodies; and worked hard drying up all things wood. Wagon frames slowly withered, cowering steadily beneath the heat and aging before their time. The narrow wooden wheels were little match for the scorching high temperatures and the wagon's constant rocking and bumping day after day, week after week, and month after month. Often the thin iron rims would work loose or dried out spokes would splinter and break. When Wagons became disabled, the train would be halted for repairs, and the making of good time became disappointment. Even on a good day we were lucky to do twenty miles, our average being 12 - 16.

Never-the-less, our Wagons moved steadily with little stopping. We rolled past Chimney Rock with the first true feeling of accomplishment. Then on too Scottsbluff with weather in our favor. It was at the Platt River moving into Wyoming, I learned the meaning of meeting the White Elephant; while crossing the river a small girl had fallen from her wagon, was trampled by the team following behind, and drowned. We buried her a good distance from the water's edge, so future floodings would not disturb her ground. She was the first of many to be buried alongside the ever-lingering tiresome trail, alone.

Each day was a repeat of the day before. Our Wagons rolled on, each excepting the self-inflicted human bondage shouldered through the dreams, hopes, and fleeting visions of a new life with promising future. Moving on from Chimney Rock we rolled past Scotts Bluff and into Fort John, Wyoming, in what was in a few short years to become Fort Laramie. Here we rested long enough to resupply our stores as best we could, then continued. Two Wagons had chosen to divide, taking the Oregon Trail North to Boise Idaho. Continuing, we ventured past Independence Rock and Devil's Gate.

Weeks grew long before reaching the South Pass in the Rocky Mountains. Staying south, we moved through the Wind River Range as land grew into a flat wide plain of sand and sagebrush. Immigrant Trains had gone before us leaving furrows in the earth; a constant reminder of their hardship and the difficulties we too would face as we took our turn at destiny. History was being made and books would someday tell our story, but for us it was life, or death, depending on the given day.

Our steady travel took us southwest across the Great Salt Lake Desert to Hastings Cutoff and on to the Humboldt River in Nevada. Here, while camped near the river we were attacked by a band of Paiute who had come down from the north. Two men were wounded, and one killed. They got away with three horses, and two Oxen forcing us to abandon yet another wagon.

While scouting, Steely and I frequently came upon gravesites and animal carcasses of horses, mules, or oxen. Often, they were still decomposing, and the stench was awful. On one occasion we came upon a human grave that had been partially dug up by some animal. Exposed were the head and arm of the victim, male or female we could not tell. The body, like some of the animals we found, had not yet totally decomposed. Part of the face and arm had been eaten by whatever creature had done the digging. We reburied the sad remains as best we could.

Passing by the Humboldt Sink, we continued southwest across the Carson Route around the south tip of a Mountain Lake, a lake that one day would be known as Donner Lake. And the steep rough trail that followed, would in just a few short years, become known as Donner's Pass; because of the Wagon Train's miss judgement of entering the climb to late and were in the winter snowfall: causing their entrapment and great misfortune of starvation. Through the hard winter that trapped them, the party slowly fell away, and for the sake of survival, some were forced to resort to cannibalism.

One week into our seventh month on the move, we reached our destination, rolling into the town of Sacramento, California. We had lost several wagons, drank our share of stale and muddy water, ate only beans for weeks at a time and baked, burned, and blistered beneath a merciless sun. We fought every kind of foe, both man or nature. Yet as we rolled single file into the city with thankfulness in our hearts and relief on our minds, a prayer of thankfulness was on our lips and a smile on our faces; for along the way, down that unsurmountable stretch of - at times - hell on earth, we had buried many of those loved and respected. Steely had been one of them, a victim of pneumonia. It was during that seven-month journey I had learned only too well, the meaning of Meeting the Elephant; we had lost twenty-three people.

In Sacramento, I found myself unemployed again. With a couple hundred dollars in my pocket, I rented the nicest Hotel room available, took a long hot bath and treated myself to a good Restaurant with a Medium Rare Steak Dinner. Later in the evening at one of the Saloons, once again good fortune found me. I met an Army Lieutenant and ended up working as a scout again, only this time for the United States Army. They were not my favorite people, but, as Big Bear had once said "to harbor bad feelings is like stabbing your eye with a pointed stick; you feel the pain, and it limits your vision."

CHAPTER FIVE

It was March 1845 I rode with General Zachary Taylor and his troops to the Rio Grande. Texas was having a disagreement with Mexico over land boundaries. Mexico claimed the Old Nueces River was where the U.S. ended their right of land, but President Polk felt differently. So, it was in April - the following month - we ran into an Army of Mexican Federales at the river's edge. There, head on, we exchanged lead and sword. It was a short fight with both sides loosing good men. That skirmish had officially begun The American Mexican War. I stayed with Old Zach's outfit for nearly two years. Again, in February of '47 we found ourselves heavily outnumbered at the battle of Buena Vista.

Five thousand U.S. troops engaged over ten thousand Mexican Federales headed by Santa Ana. The battle lasted well over twenty-four hours, and a lot of blood was spilled, including some of mine. At mid-point of the fight, I was shot in the leg and sliced across the back by sword; that weapon was not my favorite. Transported behind the lines to a field hospital, I remained several weeks until released. The cut left a scar that nearly matched the one on my chest, and my leg fortunately returned to full usage. Considering myself lucky, and with the American Mexican War winding down, I gave Zach a heart-felt goodbye and returned to civilian life.

For the next several years I worked with Wagon Trains, scouting again, gaining much more experience. I made friends, and in a short time became a Wagon Master myself. Over the years I traveled all the routes known as the Oregon and California Trails. Once, to my somewhat liking, I Mastered the Sante Fe trail down into my old home front, New Mexico; Albuquerque had grown up.

Through the mid to late fifties the railroad was busy laying track running deep into the western territories. The wagon train business was beginning to slow, so I hired on with the Army again, scouting. Working from Fort Boise I scouted mainly through the Cascade, Bitterroot and Wind River ranges. Whites were homesteading in nearly every direction West and for the Indian, this was considered an invasion upon their land. The Northern tribes like the Nez Perce, Crow, Blackfoot, Shoshone, and Paiute were becoming more and more displeased and had begun forming War Parties, making frequent and savage raids.

While scouting south within the Great Basin region, I kept my ears and eyes wide open. A fierce and hard-hitting band of renegades led by a warrior called Majahee, had been striking homesteaders within the Utah Territory. My boundary line was the Humboldt River, and I was to scout for signs of invasion within this area. The Basin range was flat and dry except close to the river. It was by far my least favorite area; I much preferred those to the North, green and wooded. But the pay was the same, and so far, the area South had been quiet and uneventful. If the band of renegades stayed farther South, that was fine. But like the wind, luck changes.

It was mid-June and a hot sticky sun beat down over the dry open range. Just north of the Humboldt Sink, less than a mile within my official territory, I spotted a large column of smoke rising from behind a distant hill. Pulling Juanita to a stop, I sat looking on. Territory or not, something was wrong. Raising her head from cropping grass, I ribbed her and headed toward the smoke.

A house, barn, and small shed lay in heaps. Nothing was left but charred wood still smoldering. With caution, I climbed out of the saddle for a look. In the front yard where I dismounted, I found a rag doll with one of its arms burned away. Then in the northeast corner of the house amid a pile of burned wood I discovered the body of a man. He smelled wretched, and I could not help but make a face.

On the North side, fifty feet from what used to be a doorway to the farmhouse, I found the owner of the rag doll. A lovely little girl with the bluest eyes, maybe five or six. Her dress was dirty, and a look of fear lay frozen on her face. Taking her in my arms, I pulled her eyes shut and broke off the arrow as close to her chest as I could. I heard the noise behind me just a second too late. As I turned, the board caught me across the left side of the face. I went down hard, the little body of the child landing at my feet.

Rolling twice, I came up with the colt in my hand, but there was no need for it. The obvious mother of the little girl sat naked from the waist up, the top of her farm dress torn away. Her feet were bare and now she sat holding her little daughter. I left the two alone, until I had two graves dug. When I returned and sat beside them again, I explained what needed to be done, the mother glared blankly at me as though incapable of understanding what I was saying; I had seen terror shock before, and taking the child from her arms for burial, was difficult.

Double saddled, we rode back to the Fort. I had cut a small slit in my blanket and slipped it over her head like a poncho. For three days ride we rode in silence. The woman never spoke once and would not eat. I prayed that Doc, back at the Fort, could reach into her mind and somehow help her, bring back her life.

*

Mid Spring found me three days into the Chihuahuan Desert. A searing sun burned our skin and sweat streaked the dust covering our faces. Scouts could find no trace of Majahee. The slow creak of leather and jingling equipment broke the silence of the desert's vain open boredom.

Majahee was a fox. He was cunning, ruthless and at home in this dry desolate land. We had a company of twenty-six soldiers, mostly young and inexperienced: one lieutenant and three scouts, each well-experienced. The heat took its toll on all of us.

It was the Army's guess Majahee's band consisted of thirty to forty warriors, every one wild, mean, and anxious to kill. They were reputed for killing soldiers mostly; but it wasn't uncommon for them to raid homesteaders and rape white women, leaving them alive to live with their nightmare.

Lt. Quiglin raised a gloved hand, halting the company. He was a tall man; big chested, brawny shouldered and head strong. When he spoke, everyone around him moved and asked no questions. He was now staring out across the desert floor, seemingly lost in thought. It was told he could smell an Indian a mile away, and grinned from ear to ear the minute he did.

Studying his face closely, I saw no expression, his cold gray eyes staring on, with no clue as to his thoughts. Slowly he took a crooked Spanish cigar out of his pocket and stuck it between his teeth. Making no attempt to light it, he continued to stare out across the open land through the heat waves dancing above the floor. When he snapped his fingers, First Sergeant Jerry O'Rorric spurred his mount and pulled up alongside him. O'Rorric was a short stocky fellow, perhaps in his late thirties, broad across the shoulders and thick around the neck and wrists. He was a seasoned soldier, and a good one.

"Yes sir, Lieutenant."

Quiglin removed the cigar from his mouth and grinned, a big toothy grin. Then gestured with the hand holding his cigar. "Straight ahead Sargeant, up in those hills, that's where the Red-Devil is, and he's waiting for us."

Together O'Rorric and I looked off in the distance toward those hills. They were the Sierra Nevada Mountains - not much more than endless miles of rock. I had heard tell from idle saloon conversation, of a couple of watering holes and a lake somewhere amidst the peaks; but I'd never been there.

I put a lot of stock in what I know about Indians and how they think, and it seemed logical to me that Majahee would have gone clear around those mountains, putting as much ground between us as he could, unless he knew Lt. Quiglin better than Quiglin knew him.

Majahee had no good cause to try and fight. Not much to gain, just thirty tired, half-dead horses, and only a few arms; certainly, no prize and not worth the risk of losing any of his braves.

Quiglin called for his scouts and asked for their opinions. All in agreement, we explained what we thought that they had gone around the Mountains, putting distance between us.

Quiglin was still grinning when he put the cigar back in his mouth and placed both hands on the pommel of his saddle. He spoke with the cigar clenched tightly between his teeth. His voice was calm, and he wore a half grin. "Well, gentleman, you have given me your opinions and I thank you; now stay close to your guns cause we're going up into those hills and kill us some Indians."

O'Rorric glanced my way and threw me a concerned look. Lt. Quiglin gave the word and the column moved out. Each of us road silent and uneasy, moving toward a destiny that if it did happen, it would be an ambush originated from the very depth of hell itself.

It took three hours to reach the base of the mountain range. A small ravine opened to our left, and I knew that was the way Quiglin would go. If we were lucky, it would ascend at a gradual grade, offering little resistance to the horses. They could not take much more push. We all knew it, but no one dared mention it to Quiglin. A half mile or so into the ravine between the high walls of rocks, Juanita stumbled and nearly fell. That was it for me; I reined up alongside Quiglin.

"Lieutenant, these horses need a rest." Anger edged my voice. "They've been pushed beyond their limits and can't go much further. "

Quiglin never looked at me. He just stared ahead. "Mr. Tobie," he replied coldly, "I suggest you keep your opinions to yourself until I ask for them. Now fall back into the column where you belong."

I didn't press the issue, knowing it would have been a waste of time. Reining Juanita around, I rode back toward the end of the column to where the traffic moved slower, so Juanita could rest a little easier while she walked. It probably saved my life. I remembered glancing up and seeing a sky full of flying specks; black spots that grew closer in seconds and pushed toward the column of soldiers with a whoosh of death. Within seconds, eight soldiers lay dead on the rocks, while the rest of us left our saddles and scrambled for any kind of cover we could find. Horses whinnied and reared, men yelled, and fear mingled well with the massive confusion.

Arrows fell like a black rain, promising a stinging death. The soldiers fired at random, not seeing any kind of target.

On the far side of the ravine, I heard a scream and knew another soldier was dead. I cursed both our luck and Quiglin. The thought of shooting him crossed my mind. By now, most of the soldiers had found some sort of cover: either behind rocks, crevices, or fallen horses. Gunfire echoed through the ravine as Quiglin screamed at the top of his voice.

"Cease fire! Save your rounds, you fool! If you can't see it, don't shoot. "

Gradually, the firing began falling off. The arrows had stopped flying too and Quiglin called for a verbal roll call. Eighteen men called out, six of which were wounded. I held Old Bear close and checked the sun. It was filtered orange and red., and I knew it would be dark soon. That would probably mean at least a couple more dead soldiers. I felt sorry for them. Most were young, inexperienced kids. I knew how scared they were: knew the sickening feeling they felt inside and understood the weeping and the vomiting. Most were just sixteen or seventeen, with this being their first patrol.

Around midnight, I drifted off to sleep; but someone yelling woke me. I opened my eyes and saw the little flames of fire shooting down from the rocks.

The fire arrows never hit any of us, but they drew a lot of scattered gunfire and kept most of the kids from sleeping. By morning, three of the wounded had died.

Except for five dead cavalry horses, no others were around. They either rode into or out of the ravine when the fighting started. I did not see Juanita and was thankful. At least she was still alive.

Sergeant O'Rorric lay 50 feet to my left, behind one of the dead Carcasses.

He must have read my thoughts, or heard my stomach growl, because after calling my name he threw me a canteen and chunk of beef jerky. I shared some of it with the three troopers nearest me and accepted the gratitude in their eyes as thanks.

By noon, the arrows were once again falling like rain, and everyone clenched tightly to what cover they had. Another roll call at noon showed two more of the wounded had died. That left thirteen of us, eleven of which were merely boys. Eleven frightened greenhorn kids against forty blood-thirsty, battle-experienced warriors. I rolled onto my back and looked up into the sky. It was a beautiful light blue with giant white clouds of every shape and size. I guessed it to be around three o'clock. Then I heard three explosions, followed by the rumbling high up in the hills. Quickly rolling back over I looked up into the cliffs, searching for the rock ledges. There they came, hundreds of them, big and small, gathering momentum as they charged. Majahee was a smart Indian, a brilliant warrior. He would have excelled at West Point. When the slide of heavy boulders finally hit bottom, they jumped and bounced like rubber balls. We clung to every bit of cover we had.

The rocks slammed into everything in their path. Men were buried alive. Thick dust filled the ravine and breathing became difficult. The entire earth trembled. I heard moans and cries rise above the rumbling; then, as suddenly as it started, it ended. Dust was everywhere and took a long time to settle. As soon as it had, Quiglin called for another roll call. Only nine of us answered. The last man to call out was O'Rorric. That was when the arrows started again, falling hard and steady, slamming into rocks and exposed bodies. This attack lasted almost five full minutes. When it stopped, we heard the hard pounding of horse hooves coming up the ravine.

Turning, we saw the charging Indians and heard their war cries. Quiglin shouted again, this time with a tone of finality.

"Hold your fire 'til they're on top of us, I don't want one round fired until they are. We'll show this renegade what the cavalry is all about. "

Pulling ourselves up we took aim and waited, like fools; that was when the arrows started again. Two more soldiers died instantly, and never saw the band of charging Indians turn and go back the way they came, long before we got a shot off. Quiglin' s voice was heard well above the pounding hooves echoing through the silent rocks.

"Majahee, you filthy Red-Devil, you'll pay for this!"

Counting Quiglin, there were only seven of us left now. Seven out of a squad of thirty men. When we had pulled into the ravine, the Lieutenant had one scout out. I could only guess where he was, or if he was even alive.

I lay back and thought about this Indian. Strategically speaking, he was a military genius. In less than a two-day period, he had killed nearly all of us and without so much as even a scratch to his own men. He had trapped us just inside the ravine, knowing we would not be expecting an attack for at least another mile or so. He pinned us down and kept us there with only arrows and three far away sticks of dynamite. Through sly and devilish trickery, he murdered nineteen men, and with little effort. If ever there was a man to be feared and respected at the same time, it was the warrior Majahee.

Night was coming again, and I knew we had to make our move. Time was running out and somehow, I knew Majahee was thinking the same thing. Just before the last light disappeared. I checked the loads in my handgun and ensured the Sharp's was ready. If I went, and I thought inside that I might, I'd take an Indian or two with me, and Majahee would be one of them if possible. Glancing up at the sky I counted seven stars. How ironic, I thought, one for each of us left alive to make a wish upon. The moon was dim, and at least the darkness of night was in our favor. Through word of mouth, passed as quietly as possible down the line, Quiglin gave the order that we would start leaving one at a time, every hour beginning at ten o'clock - with me being the first and himself the last. He used his pocket watch and sent words down by whisper when it was time. For the first time in two days, I left the security of the rocks I lay behind. Quietly, I crawled along the rock floor on my belly with Bear draped across my arms. Once around the small turn in the ravine, I moved to my feet and continued slowly - checking each step carefully.

The night was still, and the stale desert air lingered like the heat of a burning stove. At one time, I thought I had spotted an Indian sitting only a few feet above me on a ledge; but I wasn't sure. It was hard to see, and I found it difficult distinguishing between what looked like a man and some of the rock formations. I guessed maybe I'd been walking thirty or forty minutes before I reached the opening of the ravine. It was there I heard the two whispering voices: ducking quickly I froze, searching the area with careful eyes. Then I spotted them, just inside the mouth of the ravine. Two braves standing shoulder to shoulder talking. I'd be willing to bet if Majahee knew, he'd have burnt them both at the stake.

I was stuck. Something had to be done, and I wasn't sure what. While crouched in the shadows a verse I had once read from the bible came to mind; "In patience possess ye your soul." No better advice could I have been given. I'd sit right down and wait for the next trooper. Maybe between the two of us, we'd be able to get close enough for a silent kill with our knives. I waited what seemed the longest time.

Sweat trickled down my back and chest. The dry heat of night was almost unbearable, and I searched the ravine repeatedly with anxious eyes.

The Indians talked quietly. Occasionally I could hear one of them laugh. Somewhere, far to the right, a coyote howled into the night, and I thought how fortunate he was to be free. Then I caught a fleeting glimpse of a black form coming down the ravine hugging the wall. I could barely see him, and he made no sound. That made me feel a little better, since that kind of movement came with experience. When he finally reached me, I raised a silent finger to my lips and pointed toward the mouth of the ravine in the direction of the two Indians. I drew my knife and, through wordless gesture, singled out which one he was to take.

O'Rorric flashed a smile before he slipped into the darkness and crossed to the other side of the narrow ravine. I knew he would be moving slowly, ensuring he made no sound. Knife in hand, I crouched along slowly. Sweat raced down my forehead, but I didn't wipe it. I couldn't take the chance; I was too close.

I grabbed the warrior like a hungry snake snaps up an insect, sticking him twice while holding a tight hand over his mouth. His partner barely had time to realize what had happened before O'Rorric gave him the same. There, in the darkness, at the mouth of that ravine, Sgt. Jerry O'Rorric and I gave a sigh.

Quickly we moved out into the open vastness of the night desert. Side by side, we ran swiftly for at least a mile, dodging cacti, and brush as we went. Finally, when we felt safe, we stopped to catch our breath. With low voices we talked a bit - knowing all too well how sound carries across the desert by night. Our eyes adjusted to the darkness, and we could see one another well.

We weren't safe by a long shot, but the smiles on our faces showed the relief each of us shared. I asked O'Rorric if he was ready to go and without a word, he gave a nod of his head. We rose to our feet, and that was when the arrow came through the darkness, slicing through O'Rorrics neck. I saw his eyes bulge and watched as he dropped to his knees. A look of disbelief showed on his face as he fell forward - dead almost instantly.

Grabbing at my handgun, I dove for the ground. An arrow whizzed by my ear as I went down, making me swear. I didn't even have time to pull back the hammer before three warriors were on top of me. I kicked one and heard him yell; another, I hit in the temple with the butt of the Colt, knocking him dizzy. While those two laid about moaning, the third one and I were rolling on the desert floor. It was all I could do to hold the wrist whose hand was clenching the knife. At one time, the blade was close enough to cut and draw blood. That was when the voice came out of the darkness. A voice as sharp and powerful as the arrow that had killed O'Rorric.

"Stop."

Our struggling ceased, and the brave scrambled to his feet. I was half-way standing when something smashed against my head. I felt a terrible sting, heard a faint squishing sound, and everything went black.

When I came around, my eyes were blurred, and my head swam. It was at least noon, and the sun felt hot against my bare chest. My boots were gone, and I had nothing on but my pants. Lying on my back, staked out, I could see nothing but the glaring sun. Then the giant Indian stepped in front of me, casting a long, dark shadow. He stood there with his legs apart and hands on his hips, smiling. I blinked my eyes and looked on in surprise.

"Hello, my white brother." He said the words coldly.

"Hello, Little Badger," I replied.

His rugged, wind-swept face took on a serious look and he spat.

"No. it is not Little Badger, it is Majahee. Little Badger has long been dead. He died many summers ago - or do you not remember?" His voice was edged with hatred. I tried to reason with him.

"Look. Little Badger - Majahee - that was a very long time ago. A lot has changed since then."

His eyes were cold with contempt, and through clenched teeth, he spoke. "Yes, my brother, like your love for the bluecoats that butchered the only family you have ever known. You have betrayed my mother, my father, and my sisters. But because my father would have wished it, I will spare your life, providing you join me now." I lay there staring at him, not knowing what to say. He watched my eyes, and I knew he could read my thoughts.

"You are running out of time. Tobie, what is your answer?"

I sighed. "On one condition." I told him, "You stop killing innocent people."

I didn't think he would buy it but was worth a try. I squinted as he laughed, letting a glare of sun slip past his shoulders.

"Ok, my brother, but first you must prove your worthiness."

He motioned for two of his warriors to cut me loose and sent two others away in another direction. Once loose and standing I rubbed my wrists, bringing back lost circulation. The two braves he had sent away now returned with a struggling figure and stood him in front of me. I looked over at Little Badger and met his smile with a frown. He took his knife from its sheath and placed it in my hand.

"Kill him, my brother. Show us your loyalty by cutting his throat."

Quiglin looked deep into my eyes. A cold look. "Go ahead, Tobie," he said calmly. Kill me."

I thought about all those dead kids down there in that ravine. I thought about O'Rorric and Quiglin's rudeness on the trail. I thought about how close Majahee was to the knife, and about the woman and her murdered family I had found out on the prairie. I squeezed the knife tightly in my hand. Sweat ran down my neck and onto my chest and back, and I knew that before long it could be my blood. I looked over at Little Badger and grit my teeth.

"Throwing down the knife," I sighed. He threw back his head and roared with laughter.

"Tie them."

They re-tied me and staked out Quiglin alongside. Little Badger stood before us, poised and proud. "We will council tonight. Your fate will be decided tomorrow at the rise of the sun." Then he was gone.

Quiglin and I talked off and on through most of the night. There wasn't much said. I found out he had a wife and three children in Ohio. He was a graduate of Harvard, with a degree in mathematics. I asked him what he was doing in the Army instead of teaching school somewhere back east. He just laughed, and said military life was in his blood.

Majahee and his braves sat around a giant fire the entire night, talking, and arguing. They were a hundred yards away, so we could not make out what they were saying. For the most part, though, they seemed to agree. Somewhere off in the darkness, we heard the beating of ceremonial drums, and grotesque shadows stretched beyond the sitting warriors. Others were dancing and singing in celebration. And so, the night went – come morning the victors would claim the spoils. The first show of light found Little Badger standing before us. He looked down at me first.

"It has been decided, because you are my blood brother, you will be given a chance to live. You will be given back your boots, and water and food for two moons. You will be given until darkness falls to run from my best warrior and myself. We will track you, and when we find you, we will kill you. If we do not find you, then perhaps you will be lucky enough to make it across the Mojave."

He smiled a long, drawn-out smile. "But do not be hopeful, my brother, we will find you. "

His eyes left mine and turned upon Quiglin. His smile left, and hatred replaced it. "You, Blue Coat, are to die here before my warriors - a slow death. One of great pain."

"Little Badger, no!" I yelled at him. He looked at me with anger and pointed his finger.

"Shut up, this is not of your concern. "

Laying my head back on the hard ground, I closed my eyes, feeling compassion for the man beside me. I prayed God have mercy on his soul.

By noon, Lt. James W. Quiglin was hanging by his wrists from a tree. Suspended there, two feet above the ground, with legs spread and bound by leather strappings to ground stakes. He had been completely stripped of his uniform and now looked a pitiful sight. Seeing him hanging there, staring off into the distance, I guessed his thoughts to be far away with his family in Ohio.

At around ten o'clock, Little Badger's braves began to drift down to the tree and sit on the ground before him. Thirty-eight warriors had finally seated themselves before Majahee joined them. A few words were spoken quickly in their tongue. Then a warrior brave covered with war paint, stood up and drew his knife from its sheath. He raised it high over his head and the seated braves cried out in excitement.

Drums began beating again. Quiglin looked at me and I saw fear in his eyes. The warrior with the knife slowly lowered his arm and approached his victim. I watched Quiglin pull against his bonds. Like a struggling insect trapped in a spider's web, I watched the limb Quiglin was tied to shake wildly from his frantic movements. He was a hard man, perhaps even brave, but now with death so imminent, there was no facade to hide behind. The moment of truth - the baring of the soul.

A foot from Quiglin, the warrior stopped, and without touching him, again raised his knife hand into the air. Again, the party of onlookers cheered him. With his free hand, the warrior grabbed a fistful of Quiglin' s hair and forced his head down so that his chin lay tightly against his chest. Quiglin quit struggling, perhaps realizing his horrible fate, accepting what was to be.

When the warrior sank the blade of his knife deep into the flesh of Quiglin' s shoulder slicing him to the beltline, the air rang with his screams. Then moving the knife a few inches to the left, the warrior again slit him in the same manner. Quiglin' s body jerked and moved frantically in reaction to the pain. The warrior continued in the same manner until he had made four complete strips with his knife. He stepped to the side, allowing the others to watch Quiglin' s body bleed and quiver. He bled profusely for a long time, jerking, and moaning the entire time. Then finally, after both he and the bleeding had slowed, the warrior again stepped in front of him and grabbed a handful of hair. This time, with his free hand, the Indian grabbed the top of one of the strips of skin he had just sliced and pulled. Quiglin' s body jerked as he let out a scream that brought a thunder of cheer from his audience. Four times the warrior pulled strips of skin from Quiglin' s chest. By the end of the fourth time, Quiglin gave no reaction. He was dead.

Chapter Six

The sun was just coming up over the mountains, a small fiery ball wrapped in thin gray clouds. An early morning chill filled the air and dew covered the desert floor. I was welcoming the sunshine now, but by noon I'd be cursing it.

After cutting me loose, two braves stood me on my feet and held my arms. Little Badger approached, wearing a smile that went well with his arrogant walk. Standing in front of me, he spoke flippantly.

"Well, my brother, it is time. You have until tonight to think about your life, to accept the fact you are to die. Run strong and do not stop, give your hunters sport. By tomorrow's moon your blood will stain the desert floor."

I left with only the clothes I wore, and a small pouch of water and stick of dried meat. Once they turned me loose, I ran for all I was worth, taking advantage of the coolness of morning. As I ran, I formed a picture in my head of where I was. I had been through the Mojave only a few times - once during the American Mexican campaign, and twice during my early scouting days. I had a fairly good idea of where the water holes were and could guess with reasonable certainty where the scattered Forts sat. But the desert covered thousands of desolate miles and if I were to survive, I would need to make every move with caution.

I guessed Majahee's camp sixty or seventy miles north of the Weird Forest. It was called such because of the strangely shaped Joshua trees there; they would afford some shade. Also, there were Juniper, Pine, and water. The only problem was, there were also scattered camps of

Mojave Indians, and I wanted no part of them. They were a contented lot by nature, but at the drop of a hat, could turn mean and warlike.

It was nearly two hundred miles of hot, scattered rock and desert between me and Fort Mojave. With the skimpy amounts of water between the fort and myself, I'd never make it. That left me with one choice - go northeast toward Death Valley; I was certain Little Badger knew it as well.

I stopped running and looked up at the sun. It was hot as fire and had already melted the morning dew from the ground. Resting a minute, I stared out across the desert toward the direction I needed to go. It was nearly thirty miles to Barstow. There I would find water. Another sixty miles beyond, just this side of Death Valley, would be Fort Irwin — my only hope.

Climbing to my feet I began with a slow, steady run. I would run until noon and spend the rest of the day in the shade, as soon as the sun cooled, I'd run again. The odds were against me, that was clear. Not only because of Badger, but equally as deadly was the desert. The Mojave was a strange place; before noon, the wind would start blowing down the mountains and out into the vast open spaces, growing stronger until around midnight when she'd take on a sudden strange calm but grow cold, and last until morning. Then the cycle would begin again.

The more I ran, the hotter I became. The small pouch containing the little bag of water and meat slapped against my side, reminding me of what I wanted but couldn't have - not yet. By noon, my lungs burned from the dry air and my heart pounded, I craved water, and the thirst was strong. Finding shade beneath a small cedar, I took a small drink and slept. When I awoke, the sun was still up, but I didn't give it more than an hour. I was hoping to do twenty-five miles a night. If so, I could be at Barstow by the morning of the third day. There were two advantages to traveling through the desert by night. First, I avoided the heat of the day, lessening the chances of dehydration. Second, I found myself wanting to run just for the sake of staying warm.

The sun was almost gone now, leaving behind only faint shadows creeping out from the bottom of the San Bernardino Mountains. I began my slow, steady run again, thinking about Quiglin's family. If I stayed alive, and ever made it to Ohio, I would look them up and tell them that they could be proud of him, that he died bravely and with honor.

I remembered the woman I'd found lost to the world and her lifeless little girl. I understood how terrifying that raid must have been; I recalled that small Indian village in New Mexico, the Bugles and the scar across my chest. I remembered Big Bear and his family - my family. But Majahee, the once blood-brother I so loved, was now hunting me, determined to end my life.

I stopped running and looked back over the area I had just covered. Any scout worth his month's pay knew how to get back to where he'd come, as well as how to get to where he was going. Knowing this has saved my hide many times.

My stomach was empty, it craved something to fill it. Pulling the dried jerky from the pouch, I bit off a small bite and chewed slowly, following with a small sip of water. I ran my tongue over my lips for needed moisture, to help slow cracking and blistering.

I began running again. To break the monotony, I ran a mile and walked a mile. I dared not change to just running, energy was slowly diminishing and the need to be conserve energy was crucial.

Wind blew down from the mountains, crying like the sound of a lost child. It created small sand swirls, and I watched them dance as I walked and ran. Majahee would be well on his way by the first show of light, no doubt on horseback. He would reach me long before I reached Barstow, I had to find a way to avoid him. Darkness had now engulfed the desert and the only light was a sky of stars and a small distant moon. It helped, but sadly, would not last.

Again, I thought of Little Badger - Majahee. I understood his bitterness, but at the same time felt he was acting far too ruthless. Not all white men were made from the same mold. I loved him, but now I was pressed to kill him. And I wondered; what would his father think if still alive.

By morning, my leg muscles were tight and stiff. I was tired, and I knew my mind was beginning to wear with fatigue. I had little energy left to burn but couldn't stop until the sun burned hot in the sky. Only then could I change to the luxury of rest.

The sun had risen high and began chasing away the chill of morning. Time was running out for me, and I knew my hours were numbered. Another forty minutes, I thought. and I'll stop for an hour's rest.

Picking out a large Ocotillo far off in the distance, I maintained eye contact and used it as a guide to help keep me moving in a straight line. It was easy for a man to ride out here by himself, scouting or tracking, and wind up traveling in circles until his water ran out and he wound up the main course for buzzards.

Big Bear had taught us the desert was a living thing, budding with flourishing life. We had learned that certain cacti were moist on the inside and good for drinking, and that creeping lizards and crawling snakes were nourishment when edible plants could not be found. He also taught us to watch for bees, they inevitably would lead a thirsty man to water.

Still running, I passed the Ocotillo cactus I had singled out, and winked at it as I went by. It had been nearly two weeks since I had a chance to shave, and I must have looked like a grizzly ready for hibernation. A bath would have felt nice.

Little Badger would soon be catching up. There was no doubt I needed a plan, something had to be done. Giving the situation thought, an idea came to me. Ahead, several miles east, was a small range of mountains. Perhaps I could prepare a little surprise there for Badger and his Warrior. Two men would hunt me, of that, I was sure; Badger would choose his most experienced warrior and the two would ride as a team.

In little more than three hours I found myself standing in a long wide patch of tall, heavy brush. And across the way, about six hundred feet stood the foot of the small mountain range. There was no erasing my grin of hope. Studying the range diligently, I moistened my cracked lips with a sip of water.

Leaving the brush, I walked to the foot of the mountain range. Once there, I turned right following a short distance along its base until I found a spot that looked easy to climb up and offered plenty of cover once into the rocks. Pulling a few small stones loose where I stood, my dry cracking lips managed a small grin as they fell at my feet.

It now appeared I had climbed up; carefully I began backstepping into each foot track I had made walking here from the brush; once back there, I continued in that fashion right out of the patch, moving backwards a mile or so down the original set of footprints made when I first arrived. Satisfied with the distance, I turned a sharp left-face and started walking straight out from the original tracks, making that trail nearly two miles long.

After a short rest and sip of water, I made a right turn walking once again to the base of the mountain. This time I climbed up into the rocks. A good distance upward I turned right and made my way straight across the formation until I was well past the brush patch in the distance to my right. Satisfied, I broke off the limb of a stubby cedar and carefully climbed down out of the rocks and back onto the desert floor. Brushing away my tracks as I went, I made my way back to the thicket of brush.

Back into their cover I sat down and rested. If all worked as I hoped, Badger and his Warrior would split, each taking one of the two trails leading them to the mountain base. One would ride into the brush where I now waited, and hopefully leave his Pony hidden and tied there, then follow my footprints to mountain base and on to the right, he'd discover the small pile of stones believing I had climbed up, and do the same, hunting me. The other would follow the trail leading to the left then turning right to the base of the mountain, where he would automatically assume I had climbed up there in that area. His Pony would be tied at the base, and he too would climb to hunt and kill! With nothing left now but wait, I Laid down and slept.

I didn't know what woke me, but something startled me. Quietly, I moved into a sitting position and pulled up the collar of my shirt. It was growing dark now and the sun was almost down. A chill ran through me, and I shivered. I hoped I wasn't coming down with desert fever; I knew it was easy to catch and killed quickly.

The brush near the trail rustled and I caught my breath. The sound was faint, but I had heard it. Slowly I moved to a position allowing me to overlook the mountain range. My heart quickened.

Sitting atop his slow walking pony, Little Badger rode easily, studying the ground as he went. He reached the base, reigned right to stay on the footprints, trailing until coming upon the small collection of rocks where my trail ended. I held my breath as he dismounted and crouched to examine the small accumulation. He looked from them up into the mountains.

"Come on, Badger, go up". I pleaded silently, "go after me."

Holding the reigns in his hand, he stood, turning back to look toward the heavy brush path. I caught my breath; surly he hadn't discovered my plan already? Or worse, I feared he might have seen me.

Following one more glance up into the rocks, he turned, pulling his horse back to the brush where I was hiding. I swore in a whisper, and quickly moved deeper into the thickets, searching for better cover.

I found a small impression in the ground and covered myself as well as possible with a low hanging and loose lying brush. With luck, he'd walk past me or be careless enough to give me a chance to jump him.

Entering the thickets not more than fifty feet from where I lay, he tied his horse to a small cedar then walked back to the edge of the patch. Once there, he bent down on one knee and studied the mountains. He kneeled several minutes staring, then rose, pulled his rifle free from his horse and walked out of the brush and back to the range base.

I waited motionless until I felt it was safe, then carefully climbed out of hiding and moved to where he had knelt. I watched with joy as he climbed up into the rocks where my trail had ended. Glancing back at his horse tied to the small cedar - I grinned wider.

The deerskin pouch of water tied to the small wood saddle satisfied my thirst and cooled my throat. I waited a few minutes for total darkness then lead the horse from the brush and mounted. Slowly and cautiously, I followed the other trail Majahee's brave had taken. He too was on horseback. His tracks paralleled mine clear to the mountain base - to the spot where I had entered. Dismounting, I studied by moonlight the moccasin tracks on the ground. There was no mistake the Brave knew or believed I had climbed in hope of escape. But he was no fool, he reined his pony to the left and followed along the mountain base in search of a spot to secure his mount, there was no way it could have climbed with him. He would hide him then climb the mountain to find me.

Climbing back into the saddle, I reigned to the left and slowly followed along the mountain range. If the warrior was up there, then his horse had to be somewhere nearby. A cold breeze was now blowing, pushing at everything in its path and howling with a strange shrill. Dampness was beginning to form on the desert floor.

In less than five minutes, I came upon a small opening in the rocks – just big enough for a horse to get through. This had to be the place, I thought, it wasn't far from where I had climbed up and the animal would be hidden.   Reining to a stop my eyes and ears scanned the rocks, searching for sight or sound, perhaps a glimpse of movement in the moonlight. But the only thing to be seen were long thin clouds drifting past a full moon high above the peaks.

A faint rustling sound came from the rocks. I turned in the saddle just in time to see the dark figure hurling itself down. There was no time to spur the mount, the combination of momentum and weight knocked me out of the saddle, and we slammed hard to the ground.

The warrior was back on his feet with the speed and grace of a Mountain Lion and fought just as fierce. The blade of his knife was visible beneath the glowing moon. It arched and slashed skillfully but missed. He tried for a cut to the face, I blocked it following with a weight-packed haymaker to the side of his head. The smacking sound was heard through the wind as he dropped to his knees. I tried a kick and he dodged. Quickly back on his feet he made an angered face, we moved in circles looking for opportunity.

The thought of Little Badger flashed through my mind. Where was he? I moved barely in time, the blade jabbed past nicking my ear. Warm blood surfaced rolling down my neck. He lunged and I side-stepped. I wondered if Badger had discovered his missing horse yet. I wondered if maybe he was watching us right now, waiting and laughing. Without warning, the wind rose, and sand swirled wildly about us. I blinked suddenly and followed with a yell that pierced the night. The knife speared deep into my shoulder; when he pulled it out, I yelled again. I tried a roundhouse with my good right but missed. He ducked and moved away. Again, we circled. Blood ran down my arm, covering my hand and dripping at the fingertips.

I didn't know how bad it was or how much I was bleeding, I did know that it nearly disabled my arm and stung, like hot fire.

His face was shadowed in the moon light, but I could see the smile of confidence on his face. As we moved, I fought nausea. I was losing a steady flow of blood, and I knew the warrior was thinking the same thing. Twice, I nearly stumbled, and my body wavered. The wind moaned around us, probably for me; for my head was growing steadily light.

Dropping to my knees I grasped my injured arm. Pain showed on my face, and a small cry of defeat escaped. The warrior stood just out of arms reach, smiling. With confidence he raised his face to the moon to yell a cry of victory, just before the kill. It was then I fell on my good side kicking his legs out from under him. He dropped like a two-hundred-pound rock, groaning as he hit. I wasted not a second.

Straddling him before he had time to catch his breath, I gave him a hard smash to the temple; it stunned him; another straight to the nose; blood splattered, and he cried out. Still another to the temple then a follow up with the nose. Blood covered his face. Recovering his knife, I sank it deep into his chest. Pulled it out and buried it one more time, telling him that that one was for what he had done to Quiglin; but he did not feel it. He would never feel anything again.

While I went after his horse in the rocks, I bundled my bandanna and stuck it under my shirt over the wound. There wasn't time to clean or dress it, I had to get out of there before Badger caught on to what was happening. I tied the reigns of the extra horse to the back of the saddle and mounted the dead brave's horse; tapping its ribs I rode away.

I gave thought to what the warrior I had just killed, did. He found where I climbed up into the mountain but knew he needed a place to hide his horse, and in so doing limiting the chance of my finding it and riding away.

So, in search, he followed the base of the mountain until seeing the opening and there secured the animal out of sight. He also knew it would be near impossible to track me in the mountains, and he counted on me knowing I would never survive crossing them; that I would hang there somewhere, hoping for a chance to steal one. So, he used his Pony as a decoy. With the animal secured, he hid just above it, waiting. He got the jump, but not the win.

CHAPTER SEVEN

It was on the morning of the third day that Fort Erwin lay a small speck in the distance. I was weak and barely conscious: everything was hazy.

I had lost a lot of blood and was now on the edge of not caring. The safety of Fort Erwin was diminishing, in my mind, growing as an unreachable hope. I fell from the saddle. The hot sun burned down on my face, and above me a handful of hungry Buzzards were circling! A new hope, although small, rose. I loved hungry Buzzards. My eyes closed; sleep was coming; a sleep that I welcomed.

I awoke in surroundings unfamiliar. My eyes were blurred, and I blinked to clear them. I lay in a big bed. Soft sunshine filtered in through an open window. Lying there, I could hear boots on a plank walkway, and the jingling of moving wagons. Birds sang far off in the distance, mingling with mumbled conversations drifting in through an open window. Then I remembered Little Badger and my ride to reach Fort Erwin.

I had given myself up for dead yesterday - or was it today, or three days ago? I tried to sit up, and my head began to swim. The door at the far end of the room opened, and it startled me. A tall, distinguished-looking Army officer entered and crossed the room. Smiling. He approached the bed. He was an older man, colonel by rank, with a show of gray at the temples. He spoke softly and with concern.

"Well, young man, looks like you had quite a time. "

I tried to smile, but it hurt.

"When you get back on your feet again, you'd best go out in those hills and thank your friends."

My forehead wrinkled and he caught the puzzled look. His thumb raised in gesture toward the window.

Those buzzards out there. If they hadn't been circling you like they were, you would have been dead long before we found you. The sentry at the gate spotted them and we sent a rider out to look. There you were, big as life — or should I say big as near-dead. Anyway, we hauled you back, and here you are."

The thank you that was on the tip of my tongue never made it out. Another man entered the room and joined us. After setting his black bag down on the small bedside stand, he turned toward the colonel.

"Excuse me, sir, but I believe it to be best that you cut it short. This man will need plenty of rest, and little conversation."

The physician was right. I was grateful to the colonel, but all I wanted to do then was sleep. To sleep a long time - like maybe six weeks. After he had gone, the Fort physician tended to my shoulder and ordered soup broth for me. As soon as I had it all down, he pulled the blanket up about my shoulders.

"I know it's warm, but you must stay covered now and get plenty of rest. In a week or two you'll be good as new." Then he turned to fumble in his bag, and I remember hearing the soft jingling of glass bottles. I was asleep before he finished.

Doc was correct, it was nearly two weeks before I was myself again, and it felt good to be back on my feet.

Fort Erwin wasn't the largest fort I'd been to, but it was one of the busiest. Because of its location, it served as a stop-over point for many travelers heading into the heart of California. Almost daily, it was busy with the hustle and bustle of wagons coming and going. Drifters and adventurers came and went in search of their hopes and dreams. Little did I know that it was one of those travelers who would enter my life and change it forever.

I was on my way to chow when the Corporal of the Guard stopped me at the mess hall door. He was a young kid; not too tall, medium build, maybe nineteen. Friendly enough by nature, but he had a pair of eyes colder than the high snows of the Sierra Nevadas. When he spoke, his voice was deep and husky. The kind that made you take notice.

"Excuse me, Mr. Tobie sir, the Commanding Officer would like to see you right away."

Fine, tell him I'll be over within the hour." I pulled the door open and put a foot on the step.

The young Guard spoke quickly, "Sir, he requests your presence immediately, so I'd appreciate it if you'd come with me now".

I wasn't sure how to take this kid, but I felt that the less we saw one another at the fort, the better off we'd be. Reluctantly, and with a growling stomach, I left the chow hall and followed the young lad toward headquarters. I could see why this kid was Corporal of the Guard, and not just one of the ranks. He was small and gave the appearance of easy pickings, but his eyes and tone had a calm strength about them.

Colonel Kingston sat behind his polished mahogany desk, writing. He looked up and smiled when we entered.

"Glad to see you could make it, Mr. Tobie." He looked over at the kid. That'll be all, Corporal." They saluted, and he left. The Colonel motioned toward a chair in front of the desk.

"I hated to bother you, but an envelope came for you today. An envelope and a horse." He showed a questioning expression and I cut in.

"Excuse me, Colonel, but I don't quite understand."

He raised a hand in gesture. "Let me explain. First of all, this envelope came by way of a civilian." He handed it to me across the desk and I took it. "Along with it, the civilian was pulling a horse, also for you. He said a small pack of Indians jumped him on the trail and told him they'd skin him alive if he didn't deliver them here. And, as you can see, your name appears on the front of the envelope."

I glanced at it to see that it was true.

"Mr. Tobie," the colonel went on, "I hate to interfere with a man's personal mail, but this does look a bit strange. I would appreciate knowing the content of that envelope." He leaned back in his chair and waited.

I thought a long time. My privacy was something I took very personally. Then again, at the same time, it must have looked a bit suspicious. I at least owed the colonel something, he saved my life. So, giving a nod, I took the envelope and opened it. It was neatly handwritten, and read:

My Brother:

Congratulations. I underestimated you. I am glad you were able to escape us. Next time though, it will be your end. As you can see, I have returned all your possessions. My father's rifle is in the scabbard, and your pistol in the saddle bag. Until next time, my brother.

Little Badger

After I had finished reading, I handed the note to the colonel. He read it himself, then handed it back.

"Mr. Tobie, I do not mean to sound, shall we say, untrusting. But this note does clear up a few small doubts and I apologize. In fact, to show you my sincerity, you are personally invited by me to the annual Fort Erwin Fourth of July Celebration Ball. It will be held in the Mess Hall, after we remove all the tables, of course." He smiled. "And I promise lots to eat, drink, and judging from the civilian wagons about, lots of pretty ladies."

After accepting both the apology and invitation, I excused myself and walked back to the chow hall. Beans and biscuits weren't exactly what I called an Army benefit, especially at night in a close-quartered bunkhouse, but it did fill the cavity and I guess that, to the Army, was what really mattered.

I ate quickly, then went to the stable in search of my belongings. To my joy, Juanita was tied in a stall, saddle still on her back. She shook her head and snorted as I approached, and I patted her haunches. My belongings were exactly as the note had said, and I smiled. Little Badger was a hard man to figure. One day he wants to kill me and the next he returns my belongings. He had signed the note Little Badger, and not Majahee, and he returned his father's rifle to me. Perhaps inside him, there remained a bit of the young Blood Brother I remembered.

I pulled off Juanita's saddle and began brushing her down. Little Badger could easily have killed me, but he didn't. I loved him, yet at the same time, I had little choice but to consider him a dangerous enemy.

As soon as I had Juanita brushed, fed, and watered, I grabbed my belongings and returned to the barracks. If my guess was right, Colonel Kingston would have no further trouble with the warrior Majahee. He would be out of the territory, and if I was right, I knew just where he'd be.

CHAPTER EIGHT

Approaching the converted mess hall, I could hear the music flowing out of the open windows. A tingle of excitement ran through me as I climbed the plank steps. The stars were bright and the moon was full. The night air was cool and perfect for a celebration. At the door, a young lady of thirteen took my hat and tried to hide her missing tooth when I winked and made her smile.

The ballroom was crowded with people, and all the different conversations tried to drown out the band. Soldiers milled about in uniform, and civilian guests brightened the room with their colorful dress. Nearly everyone present smiled and laughed. It was a joyous atmosphere and promised to be an unforgettable evening.

I made my way to the far side of the room and found a quiet corner. A young boy passed by carrying a tray of punch-filled glasses. He handed me one. I took it but didn't get a chance to thank him before he was gone, disappearing into the crowd.

Taking a sip I threw my attention in the direction of the band. It was made up of an old fiddler, a tall, lanky fellow with a banjo, a young man with a tambourine. A bearded fellow with a guitar and a mighty fine singing voice crooned.

Merrily, I listened as they struck up "Deep in the Heart of Texas" and began to tap my foot in time to the music. It was a stirring song and had a way of reaching into a man's soul. The entire crowd was singing along, their voices and clapping filling the ballroom, spilling out through the open windows and drifting across the prairie. I was wishing it could have carried itself all the way to a small, long-forgotten

Indian village in New Mexico where I suspected a group of Indian Warriors were camped.

When the song ended, everyone cheered and applauded. The band immediately began another song - this time a slow, peaceful waltz. That was when I saw her.

She was beautiful, stunning. Her coal black hair fell with radiance to her shapely hips. Beneath the lantern light it glistened and sparkled as if it were sprinkled with a thousand tiny diamonds. Her smile was as lovely and breath-taking as a Colorado autumn. Her skin glowed with a look of softness, light olive-brown in color highlighting the magnificent whiteness of her teeth. As she talked with another woman. I watched her eyes. They were dark, shadowed with mystery and intrigue, almond in shape. giving away the trace of Spanish ancestry that obviously flowed in her blood. She was a tall woman, trim, graceful, and proud. Her slim figure was poised. She excused herself from the woman and I watched as she crossed the ballroom, moving with grace and ease.

Her long Red Velvet dress nearly touched the floor as she held a gathering of material in each hand. I watched as nearly every man she passed made it a point to turn and smile at her. When she finally reached the far side of the dance hall and stopped, five men rose and offered their chairs.

It was then that I made a face and decided she was way out of my class. This was a lady, soft and gentle and lovely. I was rough, and too often alone.

When she sat, the five men gathered about her flashing their smiles. She was courteous with each, and I wondered if she was really impressed. Whenever speaking, she used her hands as an aid of expression, and they were beautiful. Her fingers were long and slender, tipped with lengthy, polished nails.

I couldn't help but watch her face as she talked. It was radiant with life and possessed a powerful magnetism. Once a man investigated it, he was trapped, hypnotized, ready to be enslaved. Not me. I puckered my lips and frowned. The soldiers were all around her. The poor woman probably couldn't even breathe. 'Men', I thought to myself with a grin.

When Colonel Kingston stopped at my side, I was unaware of his presence until he spoke.

"Don't you think your boot has had enough punch, Mr. Tobie?"

I looked first at him, then quickly down at the floor. Straightening the glass in my hand, I felt myself flush. He cleared his throat to hide the smile on his face.

"A beautiful woman, isn't she?" Together, we glanced in her direction.

"Yes," I told him.

"She comes from Missouri, near Saint Louis, I believe, on her way to the city of Ventura. Something about a nephew. She applied for an escort when she arrived; unfortunately, I had to refuse her. Defense of the fort, you understand." I nodded.

The band on the stage began playing "Old Susanna" and I looked over all the soldiers standing about in their blue uniforms, proud, tall, and impressive. They could probably win any girl's heart simply by appearance. Somewhere in the crowd, the beautiful woman with the almond eyes stood, but I couldn't see her.

"Mr. Tobie, would you like to me to introduce you?"

Wrinkles showed on my forehead, and without removing my eyes from the crowd, I moved my head a little closer to the colonel. The music and clapping were loud.

"Pardon me. Sir?" He raised his tone above the music.

"I said, would you like me to introduce you to the young lady?" I looked quickly at him, and for the second time that evening, felt embarrassed.

"Oh no, Sir, thank you. "I put a hand on my hip and glanced down at my boots, then back up at him.

"Women and I are, well, I'm just not much of a conversationalist when it comes to a lady". He smiled, patted my shoulder, excused himself and left.

When the song finally ended, the band played "Turkey in the Straw", and everyone moved to the middle of the dance floor, bubbling with enthusiasm.

The lady from Saint Lovis was paired with a Major, covered with campaign ribbons. The music was loud and echoed through the ballroom. Feet stomped the hard plank floor as everyone promenaded with their partners. The old fiddler was right up front making that violin talk. It was a grand party, and I had seen few like it. The song lasted a long time and when it finally ended, everyone broke up in search of seats. I caught a glimpse of the beautiful lady and thought I saw her staring at me, but she immediately averted her eyes back to the fancy-pants war hero and smiled at him.

I gulped the remainder of my drink and searched for a place to set the empty glass. I couldn't find one and frowned. A sergeant walked by with a smiling lady on his arm, so I excused myself and stuck the glass in his empty hand. After making my way to the door. I picked up my hat and went out.

The late-night air was cool. A light breeze ruffled my hair, and I stuck my hat on my head. Somewhere off to my right, hidden in the shadows, a young couple was entangled in one another's arms, and they giggled softly. I thought about the woman inside. What was it about her? I had seen beautiful women before. Suddenly, I had half a notion to charge back inside and ask her to dance; and with a little luck, her war hero would object. I started up the steps but stopped.

No, I thought, wrecking his face certainly wouldn't impress the lady, and I had no desire to spend a week in the stockade. So I went in and hit the rack.

Next morning, I woke at six. Dew covered the ground, and the blanket of darkness was beginning to fade. Over the mountains, two clouds had split and rays from the morning sun filtered down, spilling over the peaks. The air was fresh, and the crispness of the morning purged my veins, filling me with a peaceful kind of contentment. Crossing to the stable, I entered the barn, fed and watered Juanita. The soldiers assigned to that detail would have eventually tended to her, but caring for Juanita was something I liked doing myself. She was a good pony and had been with me a long time. Despite her getting along in years, she could still hold her own and was now all that I had left of my family memories. The happy ones, anyway.

I removed a hanging curry comb from a rusty spike and smiled as she snorted with a stomp. She knew what was coming, and I gave her a gentle pat. While brushing her mane, the doorway into the barn darkened for only a second, and I knew someone had slipped quietly through the half open door. Someone who now stood behind me. I continued to brush, waiting. I wasn't wearing my gun. Whoever it was moved silently to where I stood and stopped directly behind me.

"Senor Tobie?" The tone was soft and sweet, not what I expected. Slowly I turned to face her. She was even more beautiful than last night. She now wore a black laced dress showing every womanly feature. She held a bright yellow shawl around her head and shoulders. Her cheeks were slightly red from the chill of the early morning. She looked deeply into my eyes for what seemed a very long time. Then she spoke with urgency in her voice.

"I have been told you are the best scout this side of the Mississippi, are you not?"

I didn't know what to say.

"Well, I guess I've done my share," I told her. "Why do you ask?"

"Because" she answered, "I have a proposition to offer you." She scanned the stable with her beautiful eyes, then looked back at me. "It will be one which will pay you handsomely. "

By now the sun was out and rising high above the Fort. Warm rays crept in through all the little cracks in the barn. Thin strips of sunlight lay everywhere.

The lady had me intrigued. Her beautiful dark eyes sparkled as I stared into them. I wondered what her proposition was, yet something told me to forget it – turn my back on her and tell her to find someone else. I guess you could call it my better judgement - perhaps a warning. But those eyes. And then she smiled. 'What the heck,' I thought, 'the least I can do is listen'.

We found a couple of boxes and sat. She was very close, and I could feel the warmth from her body. Removing the shawl from her head, she laid it to rest across her shoulders.

"Senor Tobie," she began, "four weeks ago a well-dressed businessman came to my ranch in Saint Louis and presented me with this." She extended her hand holding a small white business card. I took it and read the bold print.

Professor Henderson 's

San Francisco School of Etiquette

Specializing in Education and Mannerism

For Boys 8 - 18 years

After reading it, I made a face and handed it back.

"You see, Mr. Tobie," she began, "I have an Arapahoe woman working for me at my ranch. Her name is Spring. She is the wife of my late husband's brother. They have a small son named Stephan. This man, who came to my ranch wanted Spring to enroll Stephan in his school in San Francisco. Because I have been educating the boy myself, she declined his offer. He tried fervently to change Spring's mind but could not. Finally, I had to insist he leave. He did so reluctantly and was a bit hot under the collar."

"So," I interrupted, "a businessman trying to do business". Ignoring my statement, she went on.

"About two weeks later, Mr. Tobie, both Spring and Stephan were missing. About the same time, Mr. Henderson also disappeared". She took a deep breath, looked away, then looked back and continued. "Some time ago the Overland monthly paper came out with an article entitled 'Cap's Boys'. The story told of the stealing of Indian children and their being sold as slaves to farmers and ranchers, under the pretense that they were helpless orphans in need of a home. I believe, Mr. Tobie, that this is what has happened to my sister-in-law and her son. I think they have been kidnapped and taken to San Francisco. That is where you come in. I want you to ride with me to Ventura, to my uncle's ranchero, where I will draw up a bank draft and stock up on supplies before heading on to San Francisco to recover Spring and her son."

I let out a short whistle and shook my head.

"Look, Mrs..... Mrs....."

"Robertson", she said, "Ms. Victoria Eliza Robertson." She said the name with dignity.

"Look, Ms. Robertson."

"Victoria, please."

I looked into her eyes. "Ok, Victoria, first, you don't know for sure about this kidnapping thing. Spring could have just decided to leave her husband."

"No, Senor Tobie, they are very much in love." She was confident in what she said, "She would not even consider such a thing."

"Well, then," I added, "why isn't her husband riding with you to San Francisco?" Her eyes were filled with desperation and anger.

"Because he is a cripple confined to a wheelchair, the result of a riding accident."

"Oh, I'm sorry," I said, feeling embarrassed. I hesitated then added. "You realize, of course, that I'm no detective, just an old Army scout skilled in tracking desert trails." She smiled that beautiful smile.

"Then you'll take the job?"

When I acknowledged with a nod, her smile widened, and she reached out and took my hand. She held it tight, staring a long time into my eyes. I felt my heartbeat quicken and my palms grow damp.

Then her smile disappeared, and her face became serious. She let go of my hand and I wiped it on my jeans. That's when she put a motivational turn to her request.

"Upon delivery of both Spring and her son, Senor Tobie, you will be paid five thousand dollars."

I whistled under my breath.

"In the event that we find them. Dead or not at all, you will receive half that amount. Agreed?"

Again, I gave a nod.

"I feel good about this, Senor Tobie." she said with a quick smile. She rose to her feet and stuck out her hand. I rose, and we shook. "You will go to the Colonel here and purchase what we will need to reach Ventura. Buy enough supplies to accommodate four; my two Vaqueros will be riding with us. We will leave Monday morning at the first show of light." She turned and was gone.

The bugler sounded Reveille and a Cock crowed at the far end of the Fort. Juanita stamped her foot telling me to get my mind off the woman and back to brushing. Patting her neck I frowned. And there in the chilly shadowy stable I asked her: "Juanita, what have I gotten myself into".

Chapter Nine

All on horseback we left Fort Erwin under a cold gray sky. When the thick-logged gates closed behind us, I knew we were leaving the only true safety for a hundred- and fifty-mile stretch. It was going to be a long, hot, uncomfortable ride, and I worried about Ms. Robertson... Victoria. I had reservations about crossing the rough desert terrain with her in toe.

She seemed too soft and fragile. She rode to my left with her two Vaqueros beyond her. One was a small-framed man with narrow eyes, and a face in need of a shave. He wore his gun low and didn't have to talk of his ability to use it, that was just as well, since he could speak only a small bit of English anyway. She had called him Paco.

Beyond him, riding the flank, was the one who she had introduced as Ricardo Francisco Ramirez, the top Vaqueros of her ranch. He was a tall man of pride and rode his gray Dun sitting tall in the saddle. Twin cartridge belts crossed his huge chest, and his wide-brimmed sombrero shadowed his face in mystery. He spoke English quite well but preferred not to use it. I guessed him to be six-four easily and considered him to be no one to cross.

Trailing behind a few feet, rode a self-appointed guest. He was along as a favor to Colonel Kingston. Important dispatches had to be delivered to the California seat at San Francisco, and the Colonel felt it safer he rides in a group rather than by himself. Reluctantly, I accepted. In order not to attract attention, he traveled in civilian dress. He had shucked his Army Colt for a pearl handled peacemaker-45 which, he too, wore low on the hip. I could only hope the young Corporal of the Guard would cause us no trouble.

The safety and comfort of the Fort was three or four miles behind us when the sun broke through the hazy sky, pouring its welcomed warmth over the desert.

Most of the morning was spent riding in silence, with me half a horse ahead of the rest. I had made it clear to Victoria that I was to give the orders and make all decisions until we reached Ventura. After that, it was up to her to decide when we would continue to San Francisco.

I guessed it a five-day ride to Ventura, barring any trouble. As we rode, I searched the hills frequently, always expecting the worst.

When we made camp the first night, I allowed a small fire beneath a cedar in the middle of a brush patch. As dusk brought on darkness, Paco took the first watch, while the rest of us huddled around the fire in silence, sipping coffee. Victoria had made it and I had to give her credit; it wasn't the usual river bottom mud I was used to while on the move.

The Mexican called Ramirez lit a cigar and the gentle evening breeze carried its aroma my way. It smelled good.

A mile or so across the desert floor, I watched as the last show of light disappeared suddenly, as if it had been swallowed up by some invisible monster. I liked the night. A lot of people feared it - afraid because they didn't understand it. I found it peaceful and calm, a time when a man could be at ease with himself, chasing away the worries and fatigue of a long day. In its own special way, it offered safety and security from a world so often filled with fighting and death.

The campfire burned low, crackling and snapping, glowing softly against the darkness. Victoria stared into the yellow flames and hummed. She stirred the glowing coals with a twisted cedar limb, and it flared slightly. When it did, I looked quickly away into the darkness. I had learned some time ago to avoid staring into a fire at night, for fear of the loss of night vision. The big Mexican lay to my right, also avoiding the flames.

The night around us was totally dark now, and a million stars cluttered the evening sky. Placing my six gun in my hand, I pulled my blanket around me and pillowed my head against my saddle. The fire popped three times, and Victoria stopped humming. Somewhere off in the hills, a coyote called, and I took a minute to listen to him. Then, satisfied, I closed my eyes and slept.

The first show of light found us back in the saddle The routine was always the same. First, we shivered against the chill of early morning, and by noon sweltered beneath a baking sun.

By mid-morning of the fourth day, there began a noticeable change in the terrain. It had begun as a brown rocky, cacti-covered earth, and was now beginning to flourish with rich green vegetation. I guessed Ventura to be a little more than fifty miles north of us. Everyone was thankful the trip was nearing an end. By three that afternoon, we had found a water hole and replenished our supply. The young kid from the Fort, who went by the name of Haskins, stripped to the waist and waded into the small pool. The water was cold and clear, resting peacefully in a small rock basin.

Victoria washed the dust from her face and splashed water lightly on her hair, trying to cool it. Paco, who had removed his boots and socks, soaked his feet in the water as he sat on the pool's edge, smiling to himself. I watched Ramirez in the corner of my eyes. He had filled his canteen, splashed his face, and moved to a shaded rock where he sat watching Victoria with eyes I could not see beneath the giant sombrero.

The baking sun began settling low in the sky now, and the dancing heat waves were thinning out. A slight breeze cooled our sticky skin, and shadows began covering the mountains.

Our horses plodded on rhythmically, tired but loyal. The desert remained as silent as its five trespassers. Only the creak of saddle leather and occasional scraping of hooves on rock were heard.

Then Hell came alive. The small Apache band came out of the sand and brush, a sudden and shocking realism. I guessed there to be maybe seven or eight of them. A rifle fired, and I felt a bullet burn the side of my neck. Victoria's horse reared, screaming with fright; but she clung to the saddle. The kid called Haskins had his pistol in his hand long before the original scream fell silent, and I saw two warriors fall as a result. They were on foot, and we were now clashed together in a fight of life or death. An Apache grabbed the bit in Juanita's mouth and fell full weight to the ground, pulling her down with him. She fell to her side, kicking and whinnying. I rolled twice and came up shooting. My first bullet caught the Indian in the chest; while a second took a chunk of skull from a brave trying to double saddle Victorias' horse. I caught a quick glimpse of Paco. He had his gun in his hand shooting as fast as he could work the hammer and trigger, grinning like a small kid at a wild party.

A heavily painted warrior flung himself through the air and took Ramirez from the saddle. They tumbled through space smashing hard against the ground. At the same instant, his horse bucked and bolted away in the distance. The Indian reached his feet first and charged the rising Mexican with a drawn knife. Ramirez dropped to his back, catching the Indian with both feet in the stomach, sending him flying over his head. He gave the renegade no time for thought. Before he could regain full balance, Ramirez was flying with both feet forward. His boots caught the Indian square in the face, and he went down without so much as an utter. Ramirez landed on his back and at the same time, shot another warrior trying to escape from the fight.

By now, Juanita had returned to her feet, and I climbed back into the saddle. A word was shouted in Apache and as suddenly as they had shown, they were gone. I yelled, and we stormed off at full gallop.

I picked up Ramirez as I stormed past sweeping him up double saddled until we caught his runaway mount. Safely distanced, we stopped, turning to look back to where the fight had been. Ramirez climbed down and mounted his own horse.

Dust was settling over the area, but there was now no sign of the Apache group that had attacked us; even the dead were gone. I asked Victoria if she was alright, and she gave a silent nod. Glancing to Ramirez, who immediately returned my look, smiled.

"That was a close one, was it not amigo?"

Slowly, I let out my breath and smiled back.

"That it was, my friend, that it was."

Cautiously we continued our way, making a cold camp that night. By afternoon next day, we could see the town of Ventura in the valley below us.

By dark, we reached the ranch of Victoria's uncle, Don Pedro DePaulis Martinez, and I was glad, because by midnight, I was sound asleep in a big soft bed.

Chapter Ten

Don Pedro's Ranchero stood tall amid an orchard of orange trees. It was constructed of thick-walled adobe and regarded by many as a mansion. Massive in size, it reached three stories.

I rose at five and descended the steps leading to the downstairs parlor. The sun had not yet risen, and the large room was quiet in its predawn darkness. It appeared that I was the only one up. My boots clicked lightly against the stairway steps as I descended. Then I saw the tiny red glow far in the corner. The pleasant aroma of pipe tobacco had drifted to the foot of the stairs and lingered.

Don Pedro sat in a chair near a big picture window, staring out in silence. I had only met him briefly the night before. He was a short, elderly man. A thin mustache covered his lip adding a touch of distinguishment. His hair had turned white over the years, and wrinkles had gathered beneath his eyes. He was a quiet man, wise both in heart and mind, the result of a life of hardship and struggle. I could barely see him in the darkness, and was about to say so, when suddenly the sun rose majestically above the orchard, pouring bright light in through the giant picture window.

"Un bonito manana, Senor Tobie." he said warmly.

I moved to his side and shared with him the magnificent beauty of the sunrise over the orchard. The gold of the sun covered the acres of trees shimmering with beauty. I felt its warmth on my face and realized why Don Pedro Depaulis Martinez rose well before five each morning to sit in his high-backed chair. The sight was breathtaking and filled a man's heart with pride. Don Pedro sat dignified, covered now with the golden light. He turned slowly from the window and looked up at me.

"Please, have a seat, Senor Tobie." I pulled up a chair beside him. "It is a nice thing you have done, escorting my niece here."

"Well," I told him, "I am being paid."

A smile I did not understand crossed his face and he said, "One such as yourself does not concern himself deeply with money. You are a man of life, Senor Tobie. A man in touch with himself. You are strong, and for a man like you, there is but one thing that can...how shall I say, fumble your logic and good sense.

"Oh, and what does that mean, Don Pedro?" I asked inquisitively.

He laughed as he looked out across the orchard. "The likes of a woman, Senor Tobie, a very beautiful woman."

Breakfast was served at seven thirty, and I ate heartily. After finishing, I strolled outside into the cool morning with a good cup of coffee. Circling the house was an astonishing huge yard of rich green grass and magnificent nurtured flowerbeds. Wrapped around the entire homestead, a plantation of Orange Groves stretched for miles in all directions, there great expanse filled with chirping birds.

With every breath came the fragrance of Flowers and Refreshing scent of Oranges. A comforting sentiment filled me, and for a time it felt as if I were the last living man ambling through a corner of Heaven. I grinned at the idea, believing no man would be truly happy without a loving wife and their children at his side. The thought made me smile when the earlier words of Don Pedro came to mind.

Although I was a guest in his house, against his wishes I spent the next few days working with the hands breaking horses, picking fruit, chopping wood, and gathering cattle from the surrounding hills.

Ventura was a beautiful city of many buildings, trees, and multi-colored flower gardens. The surrounding terrain was rich with green vegetation. Cattle grazed leisurely on green rolling hills. To the city's east side, the great Pacific Ocean lapped against its peaceful shore. It was one of the most beautiful cities I had ever seen.

On the third day of our visit, I rode with Victoria to a place she called Serena Sorpresa - Serene Suprise - and that is exactly what it was. We rode by buggy to this favorite spot of her childhood. It was a giant mountain of a rock sitting at the ocean's edge where waves slapped gently at its base. Abandoning the buggy, we climbed atop the massive rock and set nearly touching, watching the slow consistent rocking of two naval Galleons anchored just offshore. Behind us, towering high over our heads, stood a beautiful range of hills covered with green grass and shrubbery stretching along the ocean's shore as far as the eye could see. Victoria was right, it was a place of serenity. With warm interest, I listened as she spoke above the crashing waves.

"Often as a child, I came to this place. It was always secluded, and I would feel as free as the dolphins playing at Sea."

She smiled staring off toward the rocking ships, "My mother would always worry over me, saying "Victoria, you are too beautiful a girl to be running off all by yourself. Someday some man will grab you and carry you away. "

I watched her as she talked. The smile on her face came from within her heart, and I knew she yearned to slip back to the past. As we sat together, we could feel the light spray of the ocean mist against our skin and taste its salt on our lips. I wanted very much to reach out and touch her. To kiss her.

"Sometimes, Senor Tobie", she continued, "my mother would send a rider from the ranch to follow me, to see no harm came of me."

A small laugh escaped her. "Often, I would hide from him until he rode in circles searching madly for me. Then I would approach him and send him home. "

Suddenly, she pointed a finger. "Look."

Together, we watched as one of the Naval Galleons heaved in its anchor and set its sails to the wind. The ship grew smaller and smaller until it had finally disappeared altogether.

"Perhaps someday, Senor Tobie." she went on, "this will be a special place where thousands of people come to enjoy the sun. "

"Yes," I told her, "And I think one day Ventura will become a city as big as St. Louis. I think, in the decades to come, that the fruit from your uncle's trees will be sent across the sea to other lands."

"I agree". She spoke with excitement, "I think that also, perhaps it will become a business as big as that of cattle."

The remaining Galleon, like the other, pulled up its anchor and soon vanished into the horizon. Victoria and I watched in silence until it too vanished in the distance. It was then she asked, "Have you ever been to Spain, Senor Tobie?"

The question was unexpected.

"No, I haven't", I told her.

"It is a beautiful country. I have an older brother in Barcelona. He too, like my uncle, owns a Ranchero. "

She looked quickly at me; her eyes alive with delight saying.

"It is a custom in Spain that a Senorita must not be left alone with her fiancée until the day she becomes his bride. The wedding is always a grand and noble affair."

So happy was she in the thought of what she was saying, she was totally unaware of the full and radiant smile on her face.

"It has always been my dream to have such a wedding, one with a guest list of a thousand friends and one that will...."

Suddenly, she stopped talking and looked over at me, her lovely face flushed with embarrassment.

"I am sorry, Senor Tobie, I did not mean to.... how can I say it.... pull down your ear."

"You didn't, Victoria." I told her with a smile, "I've enjoyed every word, please continue". "

"No, Senor, I talk too much; besides, I am interested in hearing about you. You are a fascinating man, and I find my curiosity greatly aroused whenever we are together."

I pushed my hat back on my head, a little embarrassed.

"Well," I began, "from birth until I was eight, I lived in New Mexico territory in an orphanage. After that I lived until age 16 with the Ute Indians, campaigned a couple of years in the American…", I paused briefly, realizing I had put my boot in my mouth, but finished anyway, "I fought in the Mexican American War. After that I spent my life scouting for Wagon Trains and the U S Army. I guess it all sounds boring and simple, doesn't it?"

Pausing, I leaned back on my elbows. "I remember once, as a young boy, my Indian blood-brother and I were cornered by a pack of mountain men, high up on the side of a mountain."

Her eyes were fixed on me, and I liked her watching me.

"These mountain men were followers of a man named "Cannibal", the biggest man I ever saw in my life. He had his rifle trained on us and with the growl of a voice, gave us three choices."

She stared on in fascination. "And what were the three things, Tobie?"

"Well, first off, we could have jumped off the cliff we were standing on; it was a good five-hundred-foot drop. Or he would have shot us right there in our tracks." I paused and looked up at the sun.

"No, go on." she said. "Please!"

Grinning, I looked over at her. "He wanted us to take off all of our clothes and do an Indian Rain Dance."

She tried to hide it, but the smile came, followed by a burst of laughter. "And what was it you did?"

My grin turned into a broad smile. "Well, let me say this, if I had to do it over again, I'd jump off the cliff."

She laughed out loud. "Senor Tobie, I would give a million dollars to see you do that rain dance now."

I looked over at her and, together, we laughed until tears filled our eyes.

A strong breeze blew in from the open sea and the air took on a cold chill. Victoria shivered so I put my coat over her shoulders. She looked into my eyes and started to thank me - but her words caught. Our eyes met and we stared. No words were spoken before we kissed. It was a gentle kiss, and when it was over, she touched my cheek lightly with her hand and I took her into my arms.

Moonlight was glittering across the gentle waves of the ocean when we left the giant rock called Serena Sorpresa. I hated to go; it had added an exciting new chapter to my life. Reluctantly, I clicked the reins and the buggy jerked forward. "Serena Sorpresa." I said the words under my breath with an enlightened heart. Later in years, that location we left, would one day be called Point Mugu; and would forever remain a special place in which to fall in love.

CHAPTER ELEVEN

On Friday afternoon I rode into Ventura with Ramirez. Supplies needed to be picked up, and we both felt an obligation to earn our keep, so together we hitched the wagon and rode off. As we bumped along the rocky road, we both remained silent, enjoying the occasional shade offered by the giant cypress trees hugging the sides of the road. It was Ramirez who broke the silence.

"Ms. Robertson is a fine lady, yes?"

I gave him a quick look. "Yes, she is," I said.

He continued. "A lot of men would kill for her, you know. It is said her husband fought four duels over her honor. "

He glanced off in a distant field watching strawberry pickers laboring in the sunshine, but he continuing to talk, "The last dual he fought was the one in which he lost his life. "

"Oh." I asked curiously, "what happened to the man who killed him?"

Ramirez smiled. "Ms. Robertson shot him dead."

We stopped first at the blacksmith shop and picked up two repaired wagon wheels. The general store was next, followed by feed at the livery stable. By the time we had all the work done, the sun was nearly down, and obscure shadows had gathered in the streets. The sky was cool, and a breeze blew in from the north. Ramirez offered to buy me a beer, so we wandered down to the Half Steer Saloon. The beer tasted good and went down easily.

We had drunk three mugs apiece when the doors swung open, and a dirty grub of a man walked in. He obviously hadn't shaved in months, and he stank of body odor, dirt, and sweat. He was missing a large tooth in the front, and an old sweat-stained hat sat atop a dirty head of shoulder length hair. A filthy buckskin outfit with missing fringe covered his pudgy overweight body, and a pair of Franklin wire-rimmed glasses rode low across his fat nose. Standing behind him, in single file, five silent children, ranging in age from about five to twelve years or so. Looped about their necks, linking them together was a long run of rope, tight and cutting. They were clad only in adult shirts and stood barefoot, shivering against the night air.

I felt myself grow tense and teeth clinch; Ramirez started to leave the bar, but I laid a hand on his shoulder. Following a difficult nod, he settled back, and we waited. The fat man wasted no words. He shouted at the top of his voice.

"Hey all you farmers, ranchers, and fruit growers!"

All activity ceased, and silence domineered the Saloon. Every eye turned to stare at the fat, loud-mouthed pig.

"I got me here some poor, parentless kids in great need of a home. And they are not one bit scared to work hard."

I studied the boys. Three looked full-blooded Indian, two looked Mexican, and one locked like he could be a Stephan, and I knew Ramirez recognized him.

"These here kids are good workers," the fat man continued. "They can pick fruit for 16 hours on end and never cry because they are cold or hungry. They are good boys, and in need of a home. Now who's interested?"

The barroom remained silent. Outside, we could hear the clanging of a hammer on metal and a wagon rattle by. One of the boys sniffed and another coughed. Light mumbles came from one of the card tables, so the fat man cleared his throat and spoke again.

"Only cost you $25.00 a head." He forced a quick smile. His remaining teeth were black and rotted "Its but a small fee to ask for my burden of troubles caring for these boys."

In the far corner, a chair slid across the wooden floor, and a big cowboy rose. Slowly he approached the line of boys and circled them several times, looking them over, occasionally turning one this way or that. Finally, he spoke.

"This one." he said aloud, "I'll take him."

"A wise choice, my friend." the fat man said. "He's a strong one and works hard. He's even got education. "

We watched as Stephan was freed of the rope. The big man took him by the arm, and I knew there was no stopping Ramirez. The loud click of the hammer on his pistol turned everyone's head, including the big man's.

"Senor, I think it wise you turn the boy loose. If you do not, I will put a bullet in your heart and I assure you, you will be dead, will you not?" Ramirez smiled calmly as the cowboy stared on in surprise. Cautiously, he turned Stephan loose. The boy recognized Ramirez for the first time.

"Ramirez!" he shouted happily and ran crying into the Mexican's open arms. Ramirez hugged him with warmth.

The cowboy, now filled with anger, saw his chance, and went for his gun. He was fast, but not that fast. Mine cleared the holster before he even had his hammer pulled. My bullet tore into his chest with great impact, knocking him through the door and out into the darkened street. The smell of gun smoke lingered around me as I holstered the Colt. No one else moved. Even the fat man stood silent, not knowing what to do. Stephan began crying and Ramirez held him tight.

When the sheriff walked in from the street, his eyes caught mine, and we stared. He studied me a long time. Not a muscle moved within the saloon. Every eye was on us, anticipating. The sheriff was a young man, but no fool. A double barrel shotgun lay across his arms. He finally spoke, his words directly to me.

"You kill that man out there?" He gestured toward the street with his head, keeping the shotgun pointed at my chest.

"I did."

"Any special reason?"

"Self-defense. "

The sheriff spoke to the crowd of men around him. "That true, boys?"

A variety of mumbles came from the smoky area of the tables, and the sheriff glanced quickly at Ramirez and the boy, then back at me. "I don't remember seeing you two around here before. You must be new in town. I have got to tell you, strangers make me nervous, and I don't like being nervous. I'd appreciate it if, in the immediate future, you made yourselves scarce".

He moved from the door and gestured with the leveled shotgun. No more words were spoken. We left quietly.

The ride back to the Ranchero was a silent one with Stephan sitting between us in the Buckboard; but close to Ramirez with his arm around him.

Victoria hugged the youngster with tears in her eyes. She brushed a small curl of hair from his eyes and kissed his dirty forehead. Then taking him by the hand, she led him to the couch in the parlor. When sat down, she began her careful questioning.

"Stephan." she began softly, "what happened to you the day you left my ranch?"

He shrugged, refusing to answer.

"You know", she continued, "we are going back to the ranch again soon, and you can once again ride your pony like you always do. Would you like that?"

The boy sat staring blankly at the floor, still refusing to reply. Again, Victoria tried.

"Stephan, we wish to go get your mommy now, can you tell us where she is?"

The boy remained silent, choosing not to speak; probably fear. Victoria never lost an ounce of patience.

"Stephan, you must realize that your mommy may get hurt if we do not go and get her. You don't want to see her hurt, do you? Please, tell Aunt Victoria where you saw her last, OK?"

The room was silent as we held our breath waiting for the answer. Somewhere upstairs, a servant walked across the floor. A fly buzzed near Stephan's head, and Victoria waved it away with her hand. Her face was white with desperation, and Stephan was too young to see the frustration in her eyes or feel the pain in her heart. Outside, in the darkness, an owl hooted. The house was hot, and I felt sweat run down between my shoulders. Then Stephan began to cry. Victoria took him in her arms and held him close. His crying turned into sobbing, and she stroked his dirty forehead with her tender hands. Then in between sobs, the child did his best to explain.

"The man made us go in the wagon. And then we rode on a big boat. For a long time, we rode horses across the hot land, and we came to this place, and that is where they took me, and" - he sniffed and burst into tears - "and mommy. " Reaching for Victoria, he hugged her sobbing uncontrollably.

The boy was still crying when I left the house. I saddled up Juanita and rode out. It took twenty minutes to reach town - to reach the Half Steer Saloon. Hitching Juanita to the post outside, I marched in. The room was bright with lantern light, and I had no trouble finding fat man. The children were gone now, and he was vigorously involved in a poker game. With Bear in my hands, I crossed the room to his table, and kicked the chair out from under him. He swore as he crashed to the floor.

"What in the hell blazes?" When he looked up and saw the barrel of Old Bear nearly touching his chest, he swallowed hard.

"Get up." I told him.

Struggling, he scrambled to his feet.

"Please, Mista, I don't know nonthin'."

"The boy we carried off tonight." I told him, "With him was his Arapaho mother. Where is she?"

"Mista, I got no idea."

When I cracked Bear across his face, he screamed and went down hard to his knees.

"Once more, you Grub", my face showed my impatience, "Where is she?" Again, he climbed to his feet, fear showing plainly on his face. I pulled the hammer back on the Sharps. It made a loud click. The room was needle dropping silent.

"You start talking, fat man. You ever seen what a buffalo rifle does to a fat human body? It is not pretty. One time I shot a man close range and sent him flying like a Kite, just sailing through the air with a chest hole the size of a Cannon Ball. And it's messy; so, tell me what I want to know. And tell right now!"

The man was shaking.

"Strongback, he's the one who done it. Called her his Venus of Squaws. Said she was the purdiest thing he ever did see. He had orders to bring her to Mr. Henderson in San Francisco. He left this morning with her. Honest, Mista, I had nothing to do with her. Honest."

I left him shaking. I wanted to knock him down again, but I left him behind in his cowardness and filth. As I stepped outside, I came face to face with the Sheriff and his Shotgun again.

"Sheriff," I told him, "I'm usually a man who does what the law says, but that child-stealing scum-of-the-earth in there held the key to the where-a-bouts of that little boy's mother, and I wasn't out to play games. I'll be leaving town now, so you can set those nerves of yours at ease."

He glanced through the door at the dirty, overweight man, then back at me. I was climbing into the saddle, and he looked up.

"Cowboy," he said. "My nerves are fine. I said it was strangers who get them to being upset. Good luck to you."

Following a nod, I reined Juanita around and rode off into the darkness. San Francisco was foremost on my mind.

Chapter Twelve

Victoria, Haskins and I made reservations for the first train to San Francisco. Paco and Ramirez went by horseback in hopes of tracking and catching the man called Strongback. However, in the event they missed him, we were hopeful of being in town at their arrival since the train would beat them in by nearly a day or two.

With eager anticipation, we found ourselves aboard the passenger coach half an hour before departure. Our horses followed behind in a cattle car and I was glad. I had a strong feeling we'd need them before the week was out.

At exactly 10:20, the train jerked forward, and steam blew past the windows. The whistle blew twice and soon the station was but a small speck in the distance behind. Haskins had seated himself at the rear of the coach, while Victoria and I sat together near the middle.

The train rocked monotonously rolling steadily toward San Francisco. The floor beneath our feet vibrated with the loud sound of clicking wheels filling the coach. I stared out the window in somber silence, thinking about the woman, Spring. The idea of her being in the hands of this fellow Strongback made my stomach sick. She would not get out of this unharmed. At best, we could only hope to get her back alive…period.

"A candy, Tobie?"

The question chased away my thoughts and I turned to face Victoria. Taking a small piece of rock candy from her weaving hand, I popped it in my mouth and smiled.

"Tobie, honestly, what are our chances of finding my sister—in—law?"

There was pleading in her voice, and I knew what she wanted to hear, but I couldn't lie.

"Our chances are good that we'll find her, but you'll have to understand she'll probably have been, hurt." Her face took on a disquieting look.

The train moved along with mechanical devotion, never missing a click or a roll. Tired, I laid my head back pulling my hat low over my eyes and slept. An hour later, soft voices awakened me. Victoria was talking with a Fancy-dressed man in the seat opposite her. She was smiling with intensity. Pushing my hat back on my head I sat up, studying the fellow with whom she was so delightfully attentive.

He was dressed like a prominent southern gentleman, but I had a different title for him. He was clean, close-shaven and wore a slim, well-trimmed mustache. A gray Stetson sat pushed back atop a head of brown wavy hair. His long-tailed suit coat laid over the back of the empty seat next to him: its absence exposing the fancy tooled shoulder rig with pearl handled short, barreled Smith and Wesson. A black narrow tie hung loosely around his neck to ward off the unbearable heat inside the rocking coach, and his frilly white shirt, spotted with sweat, clung to his body with a tailored fit. I'd seen men like him before; they were thick as the Muskrats along the Mississippi River, and practically ran the city of New Orleans. He was a gentleman all right, at least around ladies, I had to give him that. As he spoke to Victoria his voice was calm and pleasant with lots of smiles.

"Yes, sirree Ma'am," he was saying, "a Big River Boat departure is quite a thing in New Orleans. Hundreds of folks - men, women and children crowd the dock waving and cheering at departure. The Captain's Whistle Blows with a thrill of excitement, and a big brass band, dressed in bright colorful uniforms set the dock on fire with a majestic bravura of Music. Dogs are barking, papers are flying, people are singing, and the river boat sailors run about forward and aft taking in ropes. Such a fascinating sight to see, Ma'am, it surely is." He looked up at the ceiling and smiled extra wide, then back at Victoria.

"But let me share with you the best part of it all, it is when the boat slowly turns her nose toward open waters and you feel her rock ever so gentle beneath you, heading' out toward the deep beautiful waters of the mighty Mississip."

He leaned back in his seat now and closed his eyes. An even bigger smile showed on his face as if he were calling back some memorable event in his life. I turned in my seat and Victoria noticed for the first time that I was awake.

"Oh, Tobie", she said cheerfully, "have you met Mr.... Mr...?"

Her friend turned our way and tipped his hat. "Roberts, Ma'am, Jonathan Roberts. "

I grinned back at him.

"Pleasure. "

"And it's a pleasure to meet you too, sir. I hope you're not offended by me talking to your lovely wife?"

I knew what he was waiting to hear, so I obliged him.

"Victoria is not my wife, Mr. Roberts. "

"Oh", he said the word like he was surprised, but I knew better, "then she's your fiancée?" He smiled at Victoria, and I smiled to myself.

"No, I reckon you couldn't call her that either. "

"Well then, sir, she's just a friend of yours?"

"Yeah," I told him. "a very good friend." Victoria held back her grin.

"Well then, Mr. Tobie". he continued. "Since friendship is the basis of your acquaintance with Miss Victoria, I don't suppose you'll mind if we continue our conversation?"

I looked at Victoria, who was now unable to hide the big smile on her face as she sat turned my way. I knew she was anxious to hear what my answer would be. With an eye Robert's couldn't see, I winked, then glanced around her at him.

"No, Mr. Roberts, "I said coolly. "I don't mind at all. But best you be told, she has been to trial twice for killing her last two husbands".

Victoria's smile widened for me but vanished before returning to her now wide-eyed admirer.

By noon, Victoria had broken fried chicken and cold rolls for lunch. It hit the spot and we washed it down with warm water from the canteens. The terrain was changing. Unlike Ventura, it was now panning out into flat country stretching long and green. Cattle grazed in smooth meadows of waving grass. The ocean was to our left but had vanished out of sight. The air was cool, and a light breeze blew in through the open windows. In the far distance, mountains spotted with cedar and prickly pear climbed high up into the clouds. The train rocked along tirelessly. The conversation between Roberts and Victoria had long since died, and she now lay asleep on my shoulder, her head rocking to the movement of the train.

By seven, the sun had disappeared behind a plateau and the coach took on a chill. Careful not to wake her, I covered Victoria's legs with a blanket. The train was climbing to a high grade, and the whistle blew three times. I watched the conductor light the oil lanterns hanging from the overhead in the aisleways then I fell asleep.

The next thing I remember was the train coming to a slow stop at the depot in San Francisco. Hurriedly, we gathered up our things to leave. When we finally came to a standstill, we rose and walked toward the exit door. A voice yelled out behind us.

"Miss Victoria. " I frowned, turning with her to face him.

"Ma'am, how about dinner tonight?"

Victoria smiled. "No thank you, Mr. Roberts, I have a trial first thing in the morning, and there's a great deal of money involved concerning my late husband's estate." We turned away, moving toward the exit. I wanted to look back but didn't.

We checked in at the Imperial Hotel on Main. My room was small, with a tiny window facing the street. I looked out over the town, then pulled down the shade. A wash basin and water pitcher sat on the chest of drawers near the door, so I stripped down to the waist and washed up. Then, carrying the lantern to the bureau, I shaved.

I hung my gun belt on the bed post near the pillow and leaned the Sharps within reach against the wall. Removing a small bible from my saddlebags, I kicked off my boots and stretched out on the soft bed.

Opening the book at random, I came upon First Timothy, chapter six, and began reading. I especially found verses 3 through 10 most interesting, especially 10. "For the love of money is the root of all evil, which while some coveted after, they have erred from the faith, and pierced themselves through with many sorrows. " Closing the book, I laid it across my chest, and closed my eyes. My thoughts fell upon the five thousand dollars Victoria was paying me. I recalled the beautiful sunrise at Don Pedro's Ranchero and what he had said, "One such as yourself does not concern himself deeply with money." Thoughtfully I gnawed at my bottom lip; for certain Five Thousand Dollars was a right handsome sum of money. But he was right, money was not what really mattered here, what really mattered was the life of a small boy's mother.

Chapter Thirteen

The knock on the door woke me with a start and I found myself off the bed with the Colt in my hand before I even realized it was morning. Rubbing sleep from my eyes, I asked who it was. Victoria's voice was gay and full of humor.

"It is I, Cleopatra, come to whisk you away to that quiet little church on the Nile. Does thou have a clean shirt on hand?"

Unlocking the door, I watched as she came walking in with a radiant smile. I shook my head and flopped down on the edge of the bed while she walked to the window and opened the curtains. The sunlight poured in causing me to squint. I must have looked funny to her because she laughed. Sitting down beside me she kissed my cheek.

"You clean up and I'll meet you downstairs for breakfast, okay?"

"Sure." I told her, "I am starving."

She walked to the door, and I yawned, long and peacefully.

"Tobie," she said ready to close the door, "don't go back to sleep, services start in one hour. "

She left closing the door and I fell back onto the bed. I hadn't been to church in..., come to think of it, I'd never been to church, except for the orphanage, and Miss Thachel was the preacher there; the more I thought about it, the more it scared me.

With a rented buggy, we rode in the direction the hotel clerk had given. It was a smooth, tranquil ride taking the most part of twenty minutes. We topped a high knoll, and I pulled the buggy to a stop. The church sat in the small valley below us. Victoria caught her breath. "It's beautiful".

She was correct, the scene was overwhelming. The church was a beautiful white building surrounded by a horseshoe of giant Redwood. A river of crystal-clear water tumbled over a small waterfall between the Church and the tree line. Below the waterfall, the river's edge blossomed with a colorful arraignment of flowers, highlighting the peak of the church steeple where a brass cross glistened beneath the morning sun. Scattered buggies cluttered the front yard of the church and groups of people stood about talking robustly, waiting for service to begin.

Clicking the reins we started down the hill, my heart beating a little faster than normal. When there, I hitched the horse then helped Victoria out of the buggy. Arm in arm we walked toward a dark-suited man standing on the steps of the church, no doubt the Preacher. He was a tall skinny fellow, with a head of solid silver hair. A big bible rested in his left hand, and he smiled as we approached. I glanced at the white tipped collar he wore and wondered how uncomfortable it was. His bible, like the steeple cross, seemed to glisten beneath the sunlight.

Although the Redwood trees provided partial shade, it didn't stop one bead of perspiration building on my brow. When we reached the preacher, he stuck out his hand. His voice was deep, gentle, and authoritative, and he never once lost his smile.

"Well, Lord be praised," he said, his voice carrying over the slew of other conversations. "Congregation" he said out loud, still smiling, "The Lord has blessed us with two new sheep. "

Things fell quiet, and everyone turned away from what they were doing and began flocking around us. Suddenly, I found myself yearning for Juanita and the wide-open range. If it hadn't been for Victoria, that's probably exactly where I'd have rode.

I must have shaken fifty hands and Victoria must have been kissed by thirty sets of lips before the preacher, who had introduced himself as Brother Myers, hustled his gathering inside and took to the pulpit.

As soon as everyone had found a seat and cleared their throats, shuffled their feet, and finished whispering, the Pastor opened his big

Bible and laid it to rest on the shiny mahogany lectern in front of him. With dark penetrating eyes, he looked slowly out over the pews as if reading the thoughts of everyone.

Such a hush fell, a pin dropped into a deep well could have been heard. Several people swallowed hard (including myself) and stared on, as if hypnotized, waiting for one of three things to happen; for the word to start, the roof to fall in or ceiling to catch on fire. It seemed as if his preaching was never going to start.

It seemed all he was going to do was stare; sweeping the crowd with eyes powerful as the handgun I'd left in the buggy. Someone in the back coughed and he threw his stern attention there. No other coughs were heard. A fly buzzed somewhere behind me; probably a pest from Hell searching for a place to hide. Suddenly, and without warning, his hand slammed the top of the lectern. Half the congregation jumped.

"Hellfire and screaming damnation," he said sternly, "sinners every one of us, yes, including me," he swept a long, pointing finger across the congregation, "all of us are headed for the hot fires of Satan's eternal Hell. There is not one man or woman sitting here, who, by one way or another, has not condemned their beloved soul to that filth-loving Devil with the Horns and Pitchfork." This Preacher was intense, so much so I began to wonder if he was Ms. Thachel herself, in disguise.

"We must Repent!" he continued, and again smacked the lectern with his hand. "Repent and fight for your soul; kick damnation right back into the grave of Hell, where it belongs. "

He left the pulpit marching up the middle aisle, everyone turning in their seats to follow him. Reaching the end, he raised a clenched fist to the air, made a face, then turned storming back to the pulpit and faced us.

"My brothers and sisters," he went on, "I had a fellow say to me once", 'Preacher, the Lord don't care none what I do, or else he would poke out my eye or chop off my leg.' Following a deep breath he continued, "Congregation, you know what I said to that man, I told him, Brother, you are full of Fresh-Flopped Hot Steaming Cow Manure, 'because underneath it all you're scared of burning in Hell. You would like nothing better than to stop doing all the evil things you like doing. But you're weak, you're an infant, a baby, a small speck of sand in the giant realm of Christianity.' Every man and woman in this place can stop their evil ways if they have a mind to," He left the pulpit again and moseyed down the far end of the aisle then turned coming straight back to the pulpit. "EVERY SINGLE ONE OF US can stop our sinning; all you got to do is do it, do it for Him, do it in His name." He pointed a finger toward the ceiling, then lowered that long skinny finger at us. "If you're not willing to try, then get out of my church, because you don't belong to gold and silver and mountains and sunshine, but rather to filth, desire, death and pain."

He cleared his throat and continued, "So if there be one soul in this church who's not willing to try and cast aside his evil ways, then get up and leave, stop wasting my and the good Lords time". He fell silent and waited, staring sternly, but no one rose. His eyes burned holes in all of us. No one dared to move. Then he smiled. A smile lit up the room.

"So" he said, "no one's going to leave. Well, God bless this congregation of angels. Please open your hymnbooks to page 203, 'Give Me that Old Time Religion." Everyone rose and sang with enthusiasm.

Monday morning brought a beautiful day. Victoria and I had breakfast at the hotel and discussed our next move over coffee. It was a unanimous agreement that we would visit the establishment of the man named Henderson.

We gave the driver his name, and he took us by taxi coach to the man's office. It was a small, overly decorated affair, complete with secretary. Together, we waited in a small reception room while she made an instant appointment for us. I had introduced us as Mr. and Mrs. Jones. When the secretary returned, she led us down a hall to a door she opened for us.

"Go right in, please." She smiled and swept me slowly with her eyes as we passed into Henderson's office. Victoria said something in Spanish, but I didn't catch it. The door closed shut behind us before Henderson looked up from his desk.

"Please, have a se..." his words trailed off when he saw Victoria. He tried to pass his red face off on the stuffiness of the room.

"Please, sit down." he said. We sat and he forced a smile, looking at Victoria.

"Mrs. Robertson, isn't it? Did you come to enroll" - he twisted his face as if thinking - "Stephan, I believe it was."

Victoria looked coldly at him. "No, Mr. Henderson, we did not come with Stephan - we came to get Stephan back. Came for him and his mother. We located him the other night, and now we want his mother. "

Henderson forced a look of fluster. There was something about this man that puzzled me. I watched him closely, searching through my memories.

"I'm sorry, Mrs. Robertson", he said, "but I have no idea what you are talking about."

Victoria clutched the arms of her chair, and at the same instant I remembered. Henderson, Louis Henderson, my good friend who never made it over that Orphanage Wall. Interrupting Victoria, I refreshed his memory. At first, he looked astounded, then smiled, stood and shook my hand, happy to change the subject.

We talked for a short time about the old days at the orphanage. Recalling Ms. Thachel and how she used to snore, and of all the prankish things we had done to her over the years. We kicked around a few of the old names of some of the boys that had been there with us, and that was when I remembered the name of the bully that everyone had feared. Pete was his name. Pete Strongback. Without thinking, I grabbed Henderson by the lapels and half-dragged him across the desk. My teeth clenched. With gripping disgust, I asked, "Where is she, Henderson?" His hands circled my wrist, but he couldn't break the grip.

"I don't know what you're talking about."

Anger welled. "If you don't speak up, I'll damned well show you what I'm talking about." I turned my right fist loose and drew it back, ready to smash his disgusting face, but the gun in my back stopped me.

"Let him go."

I did, reluctantly, and raised my arms. Strongback hadn't changed much. He was still ugly in both looks and actions. Henderson thanked Strongback and slapped me in the face.

"You're a dead man, Tobie." Glancing at Victoria, he added, "And so are you. Get them out of here, Pete. You know what to do."

Half stalling, yet half wanting to know, I looked at Strongback. "Wait a minute," I said. "I've got a question for you Pete Strongback. Just out of curiosity, what happened to the Arapahoe woman, the boy's mother?"

With a smirk he looked over at Victoria. I had my fun, then traded her to a group of Comancheros. That said he looked back at me. "Now, let's go." We never did. The small derringer appeared suddenly in Victoria's hand, and she fired instantly. The small bullet tore into Strongback's heart, seeming at first to only stun him, he stood there in silent disbelief. Then looked over at Henderson and dropped to his knees, falling dead across the carpet.

By noon, Henderson was behind bars, and we had been reunited with Ramirez and Paco. By one o'clock, they had two pack mules loaded with supplies, and I was in my hotel room arguing with Victoria.

"Victoria, you're not going. Comancheros are mean and ugly human beings. All they know is killing; besides, we'll be riding hard and when we catch them, it will be like catching the devil himself. And we have no idea how many there are. It is just too risky for you."

I walked to the tiny window and peered down over the street. People were everywhere. A wagon rolled by followed by two riders on horseback. I could hear the voices of children playing and the sun felt warm as it came through the window. Victoria spoke with firmness.

"Are you through?" she asked. "And have you forgotten just who is working for who?" I turned to face her.

"Blast, the money, Victoria, we are going after cold-blooded killers, a pack of them, and I say it again, that is no place for a woman, especially for the woman I...." I caught myself. "You are not going that's all." I threw up my arms and turned away, frustrated with worry for her.

"Tobie," she said calmly, "I can shoot as straight as any man and you're going to need every gun you can get when you catch them. I've been riding horses since I was four, and I'm not somebody's old grandmother, I'll match saddle hours with you any day."

Still angry, I turned again to face her, ready for more argument; but she smiled, and impetuously we embraced.

A minute of silence passed just holding one another. Finally, I told her, "Victoria."

"What?" she asked.

"You, indeed, can be very well exasperating. "

Chapter Fourteen

We received our first lead in Dalyville. A blacksmith acknowledged he had shoed one of the horses of seen six men and an Indian woman tied to her saddle.

He told us they had mentioned riding West to a spot called Sand Bottom River, to meet up with friends; said we'd recognize it by the small, thick forest of white birch along the river's edge. Told us the water was shallow there.

Thanking him we rode out. Six men, I thought. A pack of six we could handle given the right elements. But, somehow, I wasn't prepared for only six; I expected ten - maybe twelve or fifteen at least. That's why I bought the dynamite; Victoria thought it a bit extreme, but Ramirez and Paco liked the idea.

We came upon the white birch forest around noon. A light breeze blew around us, and the leaves dangled from the swaying branches like a forest of chimes. A few pines towered over the birch, and the setting was soft and relaxing.

The four of us split up to look for signs of a trail. Haskins did not come with us. His dispatches had not yet been delivered, and he said he had pressing business to take care of, so we left him back at the hotel.

Paco was the one who found the tracks. They ran downstream a mile paralleling the riverbank, then headed off to the northeast. It was my guess Nevada or Oregon was their destination.

By dusk we had trailed as far as Rio Vista. Like the falling sand of an hourglass, night began pouring in around us. Wearily, we staked our horses and pack mule, then made camp. The Arapahoe woman, Spring, was heavy on everyone's mind. Together, we sat close around the fire, but the conversation remained as still as the night around us. Flames danced, wood crackled, and somewhere near a coyote howled. It was a restless night for all, and sleep took its time coming.

From Rio Vista, the tracks circled around Sacramento and into the little town of Grizzly Flats. They were still traveling a northeast bearing, and I was reasonably sure of their exact destination, - Reno.

In Grizzly Flats, we watered the horses and mules; then visited the local saloon. Even Victoria found the beer refreshing. A Mexican and his son boy ran the bar there. Ramirez stood talking to him while Victoria and I sat at a small table near the door. I ordered two beers and waited for the young boy to bring them. Paco was still outside, gathering as much information as he could. When the boy set the bees on the table, I smiled.

"You speak Ingles?"

"Si." he said soberly.

I took out two bits for the beer and a shiny new dollar, besides. "We are looking for six riders and a woman. I think they may have passed through here in the last couple of days."

I studied the boy's face. He did not answer, so I began tossing the coin up in the air. "The woman they had with them - they stole her. She has a small son, probably your age. You wouldn't like for that woman to be your mama, would you?"

He looked me squarely in the eyes now, completely ignoring the money.

"They were here, Senor. "

"When?"

"The day before yesterday. "

"How many?"

"They had ridden in six of them, seven counting the lady, but two others had been here waiting and left with them."

I put the dollar in the boy's hand.

"Thank you, Son."

"Senor. "

"Yeah?"

"They are very mean men, they also hurt my mother while they were here, and threatened the life of my father.

Understandingly, I touched the boy's shoulder.

"I'll remember that when we catch them, okay?"

He grinned at me with satisfaction, then turned away. Victoria was afraid for Spring, and I didn't blame her.

We were on our way out of the saloon, determined to ride hell-bent for leather when Paco met us at the door, eager for a beer. Ramirez said something to him in Spanish, and Paco came away with us mumbling angrily under his breath.

We rode hard the rest of the day. The tracks on the ground indicated the boy's truth. There were two additional set of hoofprints now, and their pace was still slow and easy. Their casual travel, coupled with our hard riding, promised a rendezvous by tomorrow evening. And by then, I thought, we would probably be in Reno.

When nightfall came, we checked into a small hotel in Loyalton, near Reno Junction. Night, I felt, was not the time to go riding in. If a man's going to get nosy, he shouldn't do it in the dark; it should be done when the light's good, and he knows where his bullets are going.

The next morning, we rode into Reno in three separate directions. Victoria was riding with me. As we strolled down Main Street, our eyes searched the scattered hitching posts for a large accumulation of tied horses. The largest number we found was only five, so we rode on past to the livery stable.

Reno was still a brisk and busy little city, even though the Comstock lode had dwindled some years back. A lot of mining was still being done but nothing like the old days. At the livery stable, I talked with the old keeper. He conceded to the fact that a large party of men had turned in their horses the night before and had gotten him out of bed to do it.

"And the cheap Buzzard Lovers didn't even tip me," he said angrily, spitting out a chew of tobacco. "One of 'em said something about the Golden Nugget, same one who knocked me down on the way out."

"Did they have a woman with them when they arrived?"

He thought and spat again.

"Yep, she was here too. Had her hands tied. That big feller what pushed me had a rope around her wrists pulling her around like she was some kind of slave or somethin'. Why, if I was a few years younger," he paused and spit tobacco again, "I'd put a matchin' scar on the other side of that no-count ugly face of his."

After tipping the old man a five-dollar piece, we left. Victoria grabbed my arm as we crossed the dark street to the hotel.

"You're pretty free with your money, aren't you?" she asked, smiling.

I patted her hand. "Yeah, but I'm not worried. It's going on your account."

Chapter Fifteen

Ramirez moseyed into the Golden Nugget first, twenty minutes ahead of me. Paco stayed outside, waiting in the shadows, and watching the door. When I went in, it was nearly midnight. Smoke filled the air, and a player piano banged away noisily – but nearly muffled by thirty or forty loud voices. I walked to the crowded bar and crammed into an opening. After ordering a beer, I turned to face the crowd. I counted twelve tables. Each filled with whisky glasses, noisy cowboys, poker chips and cards. Saloon girls made their way from table to table, smiling and worming drinks from the obliging men.

Ramirez stood at the far end of the bar. I looked over at him and saw him nod his head toward a table. The man with the scar on his face sat playing poker with four others. A cigarette dangled from his lips, and he squinted against the smoke drifting up into his eyes. I had no idea how many of his people were in there with him, or where they were located, but I did know I would have the upper hand.

I thought about waiting and following scare-face once he left the saloon, hoping he might lead me to Spring, but that would be a fat chance. I studied him. His clothes were clean, his hair neatly combed, his face closely shaved, and the cigarette he smoked was store bought. He struck me as a man who loved life and the luxuries he could steal from it. I thought to myself, 'A man who loves luxuries is a man who likes living.' I had an idea.

Old Bear was leaning against the bar, and I picked it up as I approached the table where he sat. Ramirez drew his six gun and held it under his sombrero. Neither the man with the scar nor the other four at the table noticed me approaching. I walked toward them, taking no detours. If anyone or anything got in my way, I moved them. I was hoping my hunch was right. Right or wrong, I thought, it didn't matter; when the chips are down, a man may as well do something, even if it's wrong.

Pulling back the hammer ten feet from the table, I pulled the trigger. The rifle kicked wildly, and the .50 Caliber tore through the tabletop, sending hundreds of wooden splinters flying. It left a hole you could have dropped a pitcher of beer through. All five men left the table in confused fright, giving me time to recharge the Sharps.

The piano fell silent, and no one spoke, everyone froze where they stood; all staring at me in silent disbelief. I had to make it good. I knew Ramirez had my back covered, so I talked directly to the man with the scar.

"Mister, " I said Looking straight into his eyes. "I'm going to put a hole in you just the way I did to that table. And I'm going to laugh when I do. You're a low-life, no-count, woman-stealing son-of-a-bitch. Now where is she?"

He frowned as if he had no idea what I was talking about. "Don't give me that phony frown," I said, "where is my Indian woman?" I pulled the hammer back on the Sharps, never taking my eyes off him. "You traded and got her from Strongback. He's dead now because of it, and you're next in line. "

He looked down at the long barrel of the Sharps and forced a smile for me. "Look, friend, she was just an Indian squaw, a stupid breed, good for nothing but working and bedding. I had no idea she was anybody's woman. I paid Strongback twenty-five dollars for her and he never said one word about her belonging to anyone, really he didn't." He swallowed hard and quit talking.

"I'll tell you what, Scarface," I said roughly, "You send one of your boys that are here to go get her and I'll give you your twenty-five back, but I damn well want her, and I want her now.

He spoke without hesitation. "Curly, go get her."

A bald man with a cold cigar stub in his mouth spoke from near the piano. "Okay, Boss, if that's what you want. "

"Wait!" I shouted. Curly froze, and I motioned to Scarface with the barrel of the Sharps. "Sit down at the table."

He hesitated. "Now!" I screamed.

He sat down and so did I, pulling up opposite him ordering, "Rest your chin on the table." He looked at me strangely but obeyed - hesitantly.

"Okay," I said, "now open your mouth." He wanted to tell me where to go - I read it in his eyes - but he had no desire to die. Reluctantly, he opened it, and I shoved the barrel of the Sharps into it. "There," I said, smiling, "if Old Bald Curly brings back your army, or if someone decides to shoot me in the back, there is no doubt you will come along with me, with the back of your head missing."

Curly spoke again with confusion in his voice. "Damn, Boss, what do you want me to do?"

Scarface pointed frantically to the door, mumbling around the huge barrel in his mouth. Curly quickly got the message and disappeared through the door and out into the dark street.

The next few minutes that passed were like hours. Scarface had a hard time swallowing but did not move a muscle. The saloon was as quiet as death warmed over. A fly buzzed near the piano, the lantern flames made shadows dance on the walls, and outside a horse snorted and stomped. A few of the men were heavy breathers and one or two coughed. Then, in through the door walked a woman. An Indian woman. Her hands were tied in front of her, and she walked with her head down, as if in shame. Behind her followed Curly.

"Here she is, Boss." He brought her over to the table. Scarface acknowledged with his eyes, not wanting to move his head any more than he had to. Leaving one hand on the gun, I cut the woman's hands free. She did not thank me verbally, but I saw a quick flicker of gratitude in her eyes. I was ready to ease down on the Sharps and take it from the mouth of Scarface when Victoria suddenly bolted through the door.

"Oh my God," she cried, "Spring!"

Spring recognized her immediately and they ran to one another, embracing and crying.

`Damn,' was all I could think of saying to myself. `Damn, damn, damn!' "Get her out of here!" I shouted at Victoria. "Ramirez, you go with them and stay by their side until I get over there."

When they were gone, I slowly pulled out the rifle barrel, stepping back a few feet. "Okay," I told him, "We're going to walk back to the hotel together, real slow. When we get to the door, you shout out and let your friends know we're coming. You make one mistake, and I'll blow away your heart and half your chest. Now move."

"Mister," he said coldly, "you're making a big mistake."

When the piano suddenly came on, I glanced toward it like a fool. Scarface spun around, swiftly knocking the barrel of the rifle away from him. It went off, kicking fiercely, jerking free of my hands. By the time it hit the floor, there were three guns on me.

Scarface smiled and slammed a fist into my stomach. I doubled over and caught my breath. That's when Paco showed at the door, fanning his gun twice and killing two of the three men covering me. He shouted something loudly in Spanish, and the third man dropped his gun like it was a red-hot piece of iron. It hit the floor and at the same time, I paid Scarface back, smashing a clenched fist as hard as I could into his belly. He went down to his knees, gasping for breath. After drawing my pistol, I picked up the Sharps and moved slowly toward the door.

"Hold it." The voice was calm. Near a side door, five men appeared and stood facing us, also with leveled pistols. We stood in utter silence pointing our guns at one another. The man with the calm voice spoke again.

"You better drop them guns. or both you fellers will be pushing up desert weed by morning's light."

I knew he was right. We would undoubtedly bring down three or four of them before it was over, but we would surely be dead as the result. The odds were in favor of the five. Sweat rolled down the side of my face, and I cursed our luck. If we dropped our guns now, we would surely die. To try and fight with the odds was also sure death.

"Damn," I said to myself. That was when I heard the voice behind me, and it surprised me.

"Let's even up the score a little, Mr. Tobie." I didn't look at him. but I smiled.

"Hello, Haskins." I said.

"These fellows giving you a hard time, are they Mr. Tobie?" He made a gesture with his pistol.

"Hey, you", Haskin's said loudly and with a smile, "Big Mouth." He was speaking to the one who had been doing all the talking. "Now you got three guns to your five, only there's one thing you don't understand. You should consider the odds against you". The man with the calm voice now looked puzzled and Haskins continued. "You see, Mr. Big Mouth, "I'm going to drop three of you by myself, before you even get off a round. And another thing, something about me you ought to know - when it comes to guns, I'm not just good, I'm damn good, and killing or getting killed don't bother me a bit." A look of doubt now showed on the five faces, and it was all the edge we needed.

"Look boys," I cut in, pulling my 44 around and on them. "We're going to back out of here slowly, and if you don't make a move, I give you my word…we won't kill you. So, let's face it, you can't ask for more than that, can you?"

Slowly we backed out through the door. I guessed, hoped, that the street was clear of any of their men. I believed if any had been there, they would have shot down Ramirez earlier. Besides, even if there were, we really had no choice.

When we finally walked into the hotel lobby, I sighed, turning to young Haskins.

"What in the world are you doing here?"

He looked at me casually. "Remember that pressing business I had to take care of? Well, I was wiring the Fort for leave. I'm on vacation, and I have to say, this stuff is fun."

Lost for words, I pushed my hat back on my forehead and smiled, then charged up the stairs. I found Spring in Victoria's room, and they were talking a mile a minute. When I entered through the door, Victoria ran to me and put her arms around my neck.

"Tobie, you did it. I knew you could, now we can all go back to St. Louis, and everything will be back to normal."

"Not so fast." I told her. She turned loose on my neck and stepped back.

"What do you mean?"

"What I mean is." I slowly crossed to her window overlooking the street and peered out, "it's a long way to St. Louis and that pack of Comancheros will be set on killing us before we get there." Satisfied the street was empty, I turned to face her. "Victoria, we'll be lucky to even make it back to San Francisco." She sat down on the edge of the bed, her face strained.

"You mean we've come all this way, gone through all this trouble and may not even get out alive?" She gestured with her hands saying, "Then let's reason with the Comancheros, maybe pay them off."

"No," I told her, "You don't reason, and you don't bargain with Comancheros."

"Well," she asked, "what do you do with them?" I again turned my back on her and peered through the window down into the darkened street.

"Do the only thing they understand, you kill them!"

There was little point in starting out at night; morning would be safer. Scarface wanted my blood, I knew. He also wanted Spring back and now, Victoria as well. Yes, I thought to myself, daylight was best; we'd leave first thing in the morning.

The oil lanterns lined the black street like a row of dim, blinking stars. Dark shadows lay everywhere. There was no movement in the street, and that's the way I liked it. A small moon sat in the eastern sky, nearly covered by cold gray clouds.

If ever in my life I was scared, it was now. I was scared for the women. They had no idea what it would be like when they came after us. When wild wolves are hungry and stalking prey, there is no stopping them, and they work as a team. The same went for a Comanchero. Unlike the Indian, he was a man with no pride, no compassion and certainly no respect for another. Everything he did was motivated by greed, and nothing for honor. They took what they wanted, when they wanted, and how they wanted. A Comanchero band, were the King of Killers.

I left Victoria and Spring together in their room. They locked the door behind me and had orders to open it for no one. Haskins doubled up with Ramirez, and I went to my room to think. Paco positioned himself at the head of the stairs for the first four hours of watching. I hung my gun belt on the headpost and stretched out with Big Bear beside me. It turned out I didn't do much thinking; I had fallen asleep without realizing.

In the wee hours of morning, something woke me. I thought I had heard quiet muffled voices and a scuffle of feet, but it was all a dream - or was it? Suddenly, my eyes sprang open, and I laid still on the bed taking in the sounds. It was deathly quiet; perhaps I had been dreaming. But just to be safe, I thought I'd better check. Just as I swung my feet over the edge of the bed, the small window shattered from the bullet. I rolled quickly from the bed and onto the floor, grabbing for the Colt as I went. At the same instant, a flay of bullets tore through the door of my room, tearing into the mattress of the bed.

I fired two rounds of my own through the door cursing with anger. The bullets continued entering like rain from the other side, splintering the wood and tearing large holes in the mattress. I fired another round and listened. Across the hall, the same thing was happening. They had Ramirez and Haskins pinned the same way. To hell with this, I thought. I had to see something to shoot at, so I reached for Old Bear.

Then suddenly, down the hall, I heard a kick and the banging of a door. The rounds kept coming and I swore something fierce, pulling back the hammer on the Sharps. There was little need for aiming. I pulled the trigger and she bucked wildly, sending the bullet to the door, ripping out the top panel almost completely and exposing two startled men. I fired instantly, catching one with a slug through the forehead; knocking him back against the door of the room opposite mine, and he went crashing through. I fired at the second man, but he disappeared. Then as suddenly as the shooting began, it stopped.

I scurried to my feet and ran to the door frame, peering out cautiously into the hallway. Ramirez and Haskins had already left their room, checking the stairs and back window.

With the hand that held the Colt, I reached up and wiped sweat from my brow and watched as Ramirez approached. He looked past me into my room shaking his head. Without a word, I left him there and started for Victoria's room. Ramirez called after me.

"Senor Tobie, they have Paco."

I stopped and looked at him over my shoulder.

"Damn."

Turning, I started once again for Victoria's room.

"Senor Tobie," his voice was shallow, empty, and edged with fear. I knew what he was going to say.

"Senor, they also have the woman."

Our eyes met and we stared. Placing my back against the wall I slid down until I sat on the floor. Holstering the Colt, I laid my face in my hands and sighed. How could this happen, why did this happen. I fought back tears and made a face. Then I made a promise; one I intended to keep: "You are dead Scare Face; I will hunt you down and this time it ends; this time, you will eat a ball of lead!

CHAPTER SIXTEEN

Empty. That was how I felt as we left Reno beneath a dark sky chilled-over with the frost of early morning. I pulled up the collar of my coat, but it was little more than a reflex; just an automatic thing I did, for the cold bothered me very little. The only true feeling I possessed was one of appalling hatred.

When the sun finally rose, throwing light and warmth over the dry unencumbered landscape, we reined up and climbed out of our saddles.

Near as I could tell, there were 20-25 riders now. Four of the tracks were those of unshod ponies, probably belonging to unemployed Indian scouts. They were traveling at a slow pace. Too slow, I thought, and it worried me. I felt uncomfortable and slowly scanned the area. There was nothing to see but vast openness. Nothing to hear but the whispering moan of a fleeting wind. We mounted and rode on.

'God,' I thought to myself, 'they have Victoria.' That low life, no count, scar faced animal had Victoria. If he laid one finger on her, I'd kill him personally with my bare hands. No, I shrugged with a sour face, I'd kill him anyway. I gave the maniac a lot of room in my thoughts. He hated me now as much as I hated him, but I was banking on two things; that underneath his cool, calm, clean, rugged appearance, he was Stupid, and Victoria was smart; smart enough to evade him until we caught up. And that was one thing I was looking forward to, catching up. Morning was slow in coming, and we welcomed the light.

The sun shimmered across the flat rocky ground ahead. The wind threw up occasional swirls of sand, and the air hung heavy around us.

I studied the tracks from my saddle and saw that they were beginning to pick up their pace.

Our horses were drooling and caked with hardening sweat, so we stopped for a short rest and watered them. With narrowed eyes, I studied the sun. One, maybe two o'clock I thought. Probably four more good hours of daylight left. They were in the lead by nearly that much. If we picked up our pace and followed by lanterned light through the night, we could possibly catch them by tomorrow noon. And if they stopped early, maybe sooner. It was my guess they would not be expecting us to travel on through the darkness. And if we did, then when we caught them, we would have the element of surprise. And with only three against twenty-five, surprise was what we needed.

Mounting, we rode on. We followed their tracks through Sun Valley and around the western shore of Pyramid Lake. It was hotter than Satan's hell and the brightness of the sun burned our skin red. Through the shimmering heat waves, we treaded on, pushing, thinking, hoping, and hating. We tied our kerchiefs around our foreheads to help sop up the continuous run of sweat. Their tracks began slowing down again, and I thought about it. First, a slow deliberate pace, then a quickened one, now slower again. They were intentionally keeping us at a definite distance. Why?

By early evening we were well into the Smoke Creek Desert. The sun was still out, but low. It had cooled and we were thankful. A breeze blew in, bringing with it the smell of rain. Sitting in our saddles we stopped our horses and studied the heavens.

A dreary sky festered with long, murky clouds, promised the worst was yet to come. And ahead, somewhere near Granite Peak, an ugly black sky showing quick flashes of light, promised the soon arrival of a fierce Thunder and Lightning storm.

I made a face and cursed our luck. Tapping Juanita in the ribs I started off, turning her pace into an easy gallop. It had cooled and the horses sweating had stopped. They'd had a short rest, and now, as long as I could see the tracks, we were going to make use of what little time we had left. Within three hours, the storm would reach us and wash away those tracks. Where, I thought, was the justice in life?

Around seven, we stopped to break out three lanterns. The sun was quickly disappearing, and darkness was swallowing up the desert. The rain had not yet reached us, but the clouds were very close. By the time we'd dug out the lanterns and repacked everything, blackness had totally engulfed us. A few stars burned above, but the Moon was bitterly cold. The wind moaned and howled eerily across the open desert, as if warning us of something.

Now on our feet and pulling the horses along, we held our lanterns close together and low to the ground. The tracks were easy to follow since they were making no attempt to hide them. The trailing was easy, but the walking was frustrating; we were making too little time. I fought bitterly with myself to remain patient. My temper was short, and the Colt felt heavy in its holster. I wanted very much to meet the man with the scar one more time.

Two hours before daylight, the rain started. At first, we felt scattered drops on the back of our necks and heard loud pings as the hard drops exploded against the metal top of the lanterns. Halting, we broke out our slickers.

For the first hour since it began to rain, it remained a light but consistent drizzle. The break of morning was within an hour's reach before the storm really hit. We were nearing Granite Peak now and could hear occasional rumbles of thunder. High in the peaks, we saw infrequent slashes of lightning.

I found myself thinking of Victoria. She was so beautiful. A woman of devotion to those she loved. She was going through all of this and at the same time draining her bank account all for her sister-in-law and nephew; what a wonderful heart she possessed.

It would have been so much easier and safer for her to have just remained in St. Louis. But devotion pushed her on, made her give of herself. It was an obsession with her that wrong be corrected and righteousness maintained. She was a rare woman and I … loved her.

The rain had begun to fall hard, pounding at us, stinging our skin. The wind was wild, our slicker tails and hat brims slapped savagely. It was freezing rain, and our lips were turning blue from the cold. The added force of howling wind arched the rain straight into us and we tilted our heads downward, avoid its painful bombardment. We were now struggling to see the quickly vanishing tracks.

Victoria Eliza Robertson. I whispered the name under my breath, remembering that evening at the dance; the red velvet dress that she wore, and how all the soldiers had admired her. She was lovely that night. And at Serena Sorpresa. I remembered how the wind blew softly at her hair, the warm sun and her radiant smile. She had looked into my eyes and I into hers and we had kissed. A kiss that brought to life a part of me that I had never known existed. It was a wonderful kiss and for me, will always be remembered as the most special time in my life.

Suddenly, as if obeying the raised hand of the Maker, the rain went from an obstructing resolute pounding to a soft, barely noticeable mist, the sun rose from behind the foothills of Granite Peak and the air took on an almost instant warmth.

We pulled up the horses and gladly repacked the lanterns. Then we ate a cold breakfast of hard tack and jerky. There would be no time for a fire and coffee.

Then my voice carried across the openness. Ramirez ran quickly to my side.

"What is it, Amigo?" he asked with alarm.

I stood with my hands on my hips. "Look at the trail ahead," I said, "and tell me what you see."

With careful eyes, he glanced off toward the mountains that lay ahead.

"I see nothing, Senor Tobie."

I looked at him with despair on my face. "Exactly, Ramirez". I told him, "Nothing to see. The tracks are gone".

Chapter Seventeen

Granite Peak was a Forest-Covered Mountain. Towering nearly 9000 feet, she was a green haven clothed with rich Green Pines and great Towering Oaks.

Yet despite its Godly imagery, as we rode on toward its base, my heart was racing with fear and despair. We had to find their tracks. Without a lead, there was no way of knowing their direction. We had to find their tracks soon or wouldn't find one at all. The ground beneath us was a thin layer of slushy mud, sucking and squishy beneath the horses' hoofs.

Then fate turned our way. We had been in the saddle for nearly two hours since the rain had stopped; the search to find a track was no longer a need; Scarface had left us a sign.

A crooked limb on a thirty-foot Cedar bowed slightly, giving way to the weight of Paco's body. He was hanging by a stretched neck from the limb, his eyes and mouth open, showing the pain he must have felt before they hung him. His legs and arms were missing from his body. I made a face and cut what was left of him down. We searched quickly for his missing limbs but couldn't find them. I was hoping Wolves or Vultures had carried them off.

Taking a few minutes, we buried Paco in a shallow grave, said a short prayer then moved on. My fear for Victoria and Spring was growing heavy. These men were animals – sick animals. And when we caught them there would be no bargaining, no compromising, no talking. Only killing.

We had ridden another mile or so when we found our second planted trail marker. Standing upright, still in the boot, stood one of Paco's legs. As we rode past it, Ramirez looked my way.

"When we catch him, Senor, he is mine to kill."

There was a demand in his voice, and I didn't reply. Our tempers were short, and the hunger for a fight was in the air for all of us.

Another mile of bearing straight brought us to Paco's second leg, this time leaning against a cactus.

We rode in silence, for there were no appropriate words we could have spoken. Haskins remained silent, giving no indication of how he felt. He was young and a bit reckless, but I was glad he was with us.

Another mile turned up an arm hanging by a rope from the branch of a lone cedar. Scarface was seeing to it we did not lose his trail. When we came to the second arm, I approached and examined it closely. The blood was thick and clotted but remained a bit watery beneath the crusting top layer. I guessed them no more than two hours ahead.

We ate lunch in the saddle, beef jerky and stale warm water. Granite Peak, I guessed was approximately five miles straight ahead. I still had no idea which way they might turn, and it worried me. We did stop to rest the horses around two o'clock. The three of us sat in the shade of high brush and rested our own bones. We were tired and weary. Sleep was something the three of us needed, but there was no time, nor desire.

A two-hour lead. I thought. We're close.

When rested, we mounted and rode on once again looking for tracks. The ground was drying now, rehardening beneath the baking sun, but there was still no sign of their trail. Then Haskins pointed a finger.

"Over there. "

Something white hung from the sharp needles of a cactus. We approached it slowly, our eyes keen on the terrain around us. Haskins reached it first, picked it free of the pin-needles and handed it to me with a look of compassion. It was Victoria's blouse.

I clenched it tightly in my hands and bit down on my teeth. Silently, I packed it into my saddle bags and reined on, Haskins and Ramirez following. I kicked Juanita in the ribs, and she ran strong, despite her weariness. She was a faithful pony and would not let me down. I pushed her fifteen minutes at full haunches and her nostrils blew wild filling her lungs with the air her body demanded.

An hour after finding the blouse, we stopped and rested.

Now, I thought, he was only an hour ahead. And this time, it would be us who would hold the definite distance. By midnight we would catch them, and they would not be expecting us. I smiled, and it was one of delight.

By five, we found ourselves at the foot of Granite Peak. Rows of giant pines climbed gradually up as far as the eye could see. Near as I could guess, it was climbable by horse for two, maybe three thousand feet. After that, it was too steep and thick with brush for a horse to even attempt.

A small gap in a row of thick-trunked pines showed where they had entered the mountain forest. Branches were broken off and the grass lay against the upgrade of the hill. It was an indication a small child could have found, but Scarface was taking no chances. He left us an even bigger clue. We found Spring in the pines a hundred yards from where they had entered.

She was alive, but in great pain. She lay nude in the grass, and it was obvious they had gang-raped her. We covered her with blankets, then fed her and gave her water. She told me that Victoria was OK but could not guess for how long.

The chill of the night was fast approaching. Shadows began forming at the base of the pines and the wind whispered strangely through the trees. It would be a bitterly cold night, and I felt sorry for Spring because we could not chance a fire. She would have to face her impairments minus both the warmth of a fire and company, for we could spare neither of us.

I kneeled by her side and took her hand. "Spring." I said softly as she shivered against the cold, "we must leave you here. We will be catching them soon and it will be safer. You must not build a fire. Stay covered, and we will be back for you tomorrow. They won't hurt you anymore, I promise."

She smiled as best she could and squeezed my hand weakly. I kissed her forehead and pulled the blanket up around her neck.

We left her there behind us, a helpless injured woman - hurt and scared, left alone to face the elements of a long, cruel Mountain Night. I could only trust the Arapahoe in her blood would keep her alive, for she was an Indian woman, strong, brave and a fighter.

We stayed mounted, dodging branches and limbs until the last speck of daylight disappeared. It was then we dismounted continuing on foot, pulling the horses behind. The night was bitterly cold, and the sky a dark vacant wasteland sprinkled scantily with stars. The moon was near full, its shimmering light mingling with the awful cold. Wind moved through the trees, whispering peculiar soft tones, sounds that carried with it the scent of death.

Chapter Eighteen

We saw them before they saw us. They were camped along a wide robust stream on the opposite side; fortunately, we spotted their fire before we left the woods out into a small clearing. Quickly leading the horses aways back down the trail, we tied them where they wouldn't be heard.

I felt good, we had caught them at last. Now, to get Victoria back safely without getting ourselves killed.

With the animals secured, we returned to observe the riverbank, and their camp. Lying behind a deadfall, we studied the layout by moonlight. They were in a clearing with a thick tree-line circling the camp. line some fifty yards beyond. The stream was maybe ten feet across. The water looked dark, so I suspected it was deep. Its current was swift and traveling with a noisy gurgle.

Most of the men were sprawled close together; wrapped snugly beneath their blankets. To the right of the fire stood a tent, guarded at the flaps by a small man trying hard to stay awake. As nearly as I could count, there were nineteen men asleep around the fire, plus the one at the tent, accounting for twenty. That meant four or five were elsewhere. It was obvious they were not expecting us unless it was some kind of trap. I strained my senses, listening and watching, taking in every sight, sound, and smell. If it was a trap, there certainly was no indication.

We had to take them tonight; come morning, they would be a hundred percent alert, anticipating our arrival.

In whispers we formulated our plan. Under rifle cover from Haskins behind the deadfall, Ramirez and I would cross the stream. He would circle around and take position on the far side of the camp in the tree line. I would move to the right along the bank in line with the tent. If Victoria was in there, I would make a slit and take her out.

A hundred yards down from the site, we slipped noiselessly into the cold water. The wind was chilling and strong, rippling the surface. I held Bear out of the water as I crossed, high enough to stay dry but low enough to not be seen.

Victoria must be frightened, I thought. I wondered if she had witnessed what they had done to Spring. If she had, it must have been a dreadful sight for her to watch, especially since she and Spring were so close. And Paco - had she seen that too? And worse yet – I thought with my heart pounding with hatred - what if when they had so savagely raped Spring, they….

Suddenly, I found myself out of the cold water and at the bank of the river. Cautiously I rose far enough to observe the camp. All was quiet except for chirping of crickets.

By now Ramirez would be in place on the far side of the camp. The dark water behind me gurgled and I could feel my heart pounding in my temples. Hurriedly, I scurried up the embankment. Crouching low, I crossed the clearing, stopping twenty or so feet behind the tent. Crouching low, I took in the sounds around me.

With eyes accustomed to the dark, I studied their camp in the same manner a hawk studies prey. Then, moving swiftly and noiselessly, I moved to the back of the tent.

It was slow and tedious; I wanted so much to move faster, to get to Victoria, but I knew better. One mistake, that was all it would take. I could easily see the yellow flames of their fire. And I wondered, where were those five men not accounted for. Just short of the tent, I stopped again, crouched in the dark shadows.

Men rolled restlessly in their blankets. The fire snapped and danced; beginning to burn low. The guard at the tent flaps, had left his position and was approaching the fire with more wood. That was when the deep voice came from inside the tent. I could not distinguish what was said, but another man inside, told him shut up and be quiet. Now I noticed a small bulge on the right side of the canvas - and one to the left as well. I couldn't tell for sure, but I thought I saw one to the rear. That explained the missing men. It was a trap of hidden guns.

I frowned, feeling anger rise again, and wondered, if not in the tent, where was Victoria?

Leaving the crowded tent to the men inside it, I bit at my lip moving back away from the trap and into the woods. So, it had been a trap after all. The moment I'd have touched that tent, they would have filled me with enough lead to kill an elephant. I thanked my luck. Once deep enough into the trees, I began moving through the trees to where Ramirez had positioned himself.

When he saw me, he approached excitedly with whispers, explained what he had seen. "Senor Tobie, they have a small corral near where I came across. It has two guards and with them is Victoria."

I looked at him, hope in my eyes. "Great find, Ramirez, let's go get her." He smiled in the moonlight, and we left together in silence.

They were there alright, sitting alongside one another, smoking. To their right was Victoria, lying on a blanket, her arms wrapped and tied around a small oak. She lay with her head resting on her arm; I could not tell if she was asleep or awake. Like two hungry foxes, we circled steadily, putting ourselves in line with their backs. With silence, caution, and nerves at a high, we crept up behind them; then together sank our knives deep into their hearts. They were dead even before we let them slip to the ground.

I moved swiftly to Victoria and woke her. She looked up momentarily startled. "Oh, my God above, "she said almost crying, "thank heaven you found us" She paused a moment and started to speak again, "Spring! They...." I put a soft hand over her mouth,"

It's OK, we found her. She is waiting for us."

I cut her hands loose, and we embraced, never wanting to let go. The only thing she wore above her waist was a dirty slip top, so I helped her into my coat. Dawn was coming quickly, and I guessed it to be near five in the morning.

The sky was a light gray, and the stars were slowly dwindling. Frost covered the ground like light snow, glistening like silver beneath the moonlight. It was cold and we could see our breath. Ramirez knelt beside us.

"What do you think, Senor, do we turn their horses loose?" He stared in the darkness waiting patiently for my answer.

"No." I said thoughtfully, "for one thing, twenty-five horses would make too much noise, and we don't have the time to hand-lead them away. It will be daylight any minute; we must get back to Haskins."

By the time we reached the edge of the river, it was noticeably lighter. Only three stars remained in the sky, and I knew the guard at the tent would soon awaken the sleeping crew.

We lowered ourselves into the cold water and worked against the strong current. Once on the other side, we moved quickly to the cover of the deadfall. Haskins saw Victoria and tipped his hat.

"Howdy, Ma'am, good to see you. "

"Haskins", I said with a rush. He glanced at me quickly.

"Yes sir, Mr. Tobie?"

I spoke without taking my eyes from the camp across the river.

"Run like the devil himself was after you and get back to the horses. I turned and looked him straight in the yes, "break out the twelve sticks of dynamite and get them here fast. If you do not, it will be too late."

He left, smiling. "On my way, I just love loud noise".

"Ramirez." I said, turning to him.

"Si, Senor?"

"Go to our right along the riverbank and find cover. Make it a place where you can hear shots coming from that tent and when men start scrambling out of their bedrolls you start shooting, making every shot count. "

"Si, Senor Tobie." He left quickly, moving first into the woods behind us. Dawn was breaking now, and light began filtering through the trees. Dynamite was our only chance. Without it, we were dead, and equally important was the element of surprise. I glanced nervously over my shoulder.

"Come on Haskins?"

The campfire had died, and the sun broke over the trees behind them, but had not yet stretched far enough to reach the clearing. I knew when it did, they would start rolling free of their blankets.

"Damn it," I said half out loud, "where the hell is Haskins?"

"Right behind you."

I turned quickly to face him and took the dynamite from his hands. "Ok." I told him. "Take your rifle to the left of us and find cover. When the shooting starts, don't miss."

He looked quickly at me smiling again, "Me Miss? Surely, you're joking, Mr. Tobie."

"Get going." I told him, knowing his not missing was more truth than fiction.

He turned to leave and stopped. "Oh," he said quickly. "you'll need these." He tossed me the box of matches and disappeared like a flash of light into the darkness. I began searching the ground for a stone to throw while Victoria made ready a match to strike. My hands slid along the dampened earth frantically but turned up nothing. The tip of the sun suddenly rose, and the newborn light of early morning began reaching out toward the Comanchero camp. We were not yet ready.

By now their fire had died and the sun broke over the trees behind them, but not yet stretching far enough to reach the clearing. I knew when it did, they would start tolling free of their blankets.

"Damn it," I said half out loud, "where the hell is Haskins?"

"Right behind you."

I turned quickly to face him and took the dynamite from his hands. "Ok." I told him. "take your rifle to the left of us and find cover. When the shooting starts, don't miss."

He looked quickly at me smiling, "Me? Miss? Surely you're joking, Mr. Tobie."

"Get going." I told him amusedly.

He turned to leave and stopped. "Oh," he said quickly. "you'll need these." I took the box of matches and he disappeared like a flash of light. I searched the grass for a stone to throw while Victoria made ready a match. My hands slid along the dampened ground frantically, but turned up nothing. The sun suddenly rose to its peak and the newborn light of early morning covered the Comanchero camp radiantly.

CHAPTER NINETEEN

Like a lucky Bullet, I found it, a small rock just the size I needed. Men began to stir in their blankets.

"Ok, Victoria." my words were coming fast, fighting against time. "Light the first stick. The minute you do, hand it to me and light another. "

With force and crude accuracy, I hurdled the rock I had found. I missed the tent completely, but it struck the face of the guard standing in front of the flaps. He dropped his Winchester yelling out in pain while falling backward onto the tent. Instantly, the tent lit up with the gunfire of light and lead. While all this was happening, I took the burning stick of dynamite from Victoria and threw it, aiming for the heart of the campfire. We watched as it tumbled through the shadowy early morning light, arching across the river and landing almost dead-on target. At the same time, men were scrambling madly to their feet in confusion, grabbing for boots and guns.

To our right and left we heard the continuous rifle fire of Ramirez and Haskins. Faintly, from the crowd of disoriented men, we heard the word "dynamite" yelled. That was when it landed with a great explosion. The ground shook, men screamed, and flying debris flew everywhere, some splashing hard into the river in front of us. I threw my second stick and followed with a third and a fourth. The explosions were wide apart but almost simultaneous. After the fifth I grabbed Victoria's wrist.

"That's enough. " Low behind the protection of the fallen tree, we waited for the last of the debris to settle. When it did, we observed the remains of the campsite with careful, sweeping eyes.

A giant hole now lay where the tent once stood. Smoke and dust lingered in the air and scattered bodies lay in every direction.

A quiet morning breeze blew the lingering smoke across the river and over our heads. It carried with it a detesting odor, one of burned wood and human flesh. I didn't believe anyone was left alive, but there was the possibility a few may have made it from the clearing into the safety of the woods.

Leaving Victoria behind the deadfall, Haskins and I crossed the stream under the watchful eye of Ramirez. Once across, he joined us, and together we searched the camp trying for a body count. It turned out to be impossible, but as near as we could guess, no one had made it out alive.

We left their remains for the wolves, coyotes, and vultures. After choosing a horse for Victoria and hopefully, Spring, we turned the rest loose among the trees and began our slow descent down the steep slope of Granite Peak - in the direction of home.

A hot afternoon sun found us riding up on the silent body of Spring. Since first spotting her, she had not moved, and our hearts began to fill with despair. Victoria left her saddle quickly and ran to her side, calling her name. She took the woman's head gently in her arms and cradled it against her lap. Tears streamed from her eyes as she held the motionless body of her sister-in-law. Then suddenly, Spring opened her eyes and smiled.

"Morning!" Victoria jumped, both startled and angry.

"Spring," she said with exasperation, "you... you..." her words stuck in her throat and more tears fell, showing the joy in her heart.

We made a small fire and cooked a quick light meal that did wonders for Spring. While Victoria fed her, Haskins and I made a travois to pull behind his horse. It would have been a bumpy ride, but it was the best we could do.

When it was finally made and fastened in place, we carefully laid Spring onto it and covered her with a blanket. Then, together, all of us happy, we rode down the mountain toward home.

As we left the last of the pines behind and rode out into the open desert floor, I was thinking to myself how beautiful this day was.

I thought about New Mexico, cattle, and especially, Victoria. Even out here beneath a baking sun that robbed most women of their soft complexion and burned red their tender feminine skin, to me, she was as beautiful as the first day I saw her.

Our horses ambered at a slow easy pace while we sat in our saddles, tired but joyful.

Reaching out, I took Victoria's hand, and she looked into my eyes. There was joy in them, a loving passionate fire of joy, the kind of happiness that comes from the Grand Maker above. I couldn't stop myself saying those words. "I love you".

"And I love you". She said with a warm, warm smile.

The shot rang out from the far distant trees behind us, and I could almost hear the bullet rushing across the desert floor. It was only a split-second thing, then it was here.

Juanita whinnied wildly, almost screaming, as she went down, falling hard on her left side. I rolled free and crawled to her quickly. The bullet had gone in just behind the saddle and now blood ran down her side. Her belly heaved and fell quickly, fighting frantically, trying to chase away the approaching death she and I both knew was coming. There was no saving her. and I knew it.

More shots came from the distant trees, but we were far enough away for most to not reach its target. It was only by chance this one had reached Juanita.

I knelt beside her head and rubbed her neck. She always liked that. Her big, frightened eyes watched me, and I knew that they were saying to me the same thing mine told her; I love you. Her breathing quit as suddenly as the bullet that had killed her. She was dead.

A small figure stood in the clearing now just outside the Pines. He was tiny at this distance, but nevertheless visible, just as visible as the scar he wore on the side of his face. His rifle cracked repeatedly as he tried his luck with Kentucky windage.

"Let me go get him, Mr. Tobie." There was anger in Haskin's voice.

"No," shouted Ramirez, "he is mine. "

"Hold it, the both of you, that's what he wants; you wouldn't get fifty yards. I'll take care of this for all of us, from right here. "

I slipped Old Bear out of its scabbard and laid down on the ground behind Juanita's body.

"No." I said talking to no one in particular, "Juanita and I will take care of this, right now."

With the rifle barrel resting across Juanita's lifeless form, I took careful, steady aim. I would only get one chance before he remembered that I carried a Buffalo rifle. Gingerly, I began my slow squeeze on the trigger.

"A Sharps Buffalo rifle," I said half out loud, "with a range almost twice that of a Winchester and three times the killing force."

The gun jerked wildly, leaving Juanita's body for only a second. It bellowed smoke, and the big slug of lead whistled through the air. Together, we watched the tiny figure far off in the distance. And when the loud crack of the rifle fell silent, so did Juanita's killer. But just to be safe, I put two more bullets into him.

After stripping Juanita of my belongings, I kissed her forehead and didn't try to hide my tears.

I saddled up the spare Horse we had tagging along for Spring, had she been able to ride. The sun burned hot, and the travois continued digging furrows into the desert ground, and behind us, over the edge of the pines, buzzards circled with hungry eyes. I glanced at Ramirez, "You know my friend, after they eat him, they will get sick or die".

Ramirez gave a nod. "See. The buzzard will eat anything that is dead, but I tell you, it will take only one bite of that man's Body, and they will kill themselves".

A family of wild quail ran across the trail in front of us, and off in the distance heat waves danced their trickery. The Sun burned hotter, but a slight breeze gave us a small bit of relief, greatly appreciated.

I thought about Juanita. I would surely miss her. She was all that had been left of my past, except for Little Badger, and his days were numbered since he had changed his name and so wrongly adjusted his attitude. Before the year was out, the Army would catch him, and he would no doubt hang. So, I thought, with Juanita gone, so was my past.

We made camp early that night, and by the time darkness encircled us, our warm fire flickered and danced against a light evening breeze. I sat off by myself watching the stars. The night sky was filled with a million stars, and a bright full Moon added to the Desert's enchantment, yet, for me, it helped very little in easing the melancholy weighing heavy on my Heart.

"A beautiful night, isn't it?" Smiling, Victoria sat down beside me. "What are you thinking about, Tobie?" she asked, handing me a cup of coffee.

Taking the cup, I answered her while looking out across the open desert. "Oh, just things I've done and things that have happened to me over the years; the sky, the night, stars, people, and especially you".

"Me," she said, smiling again. "What about me?"

I returned her smile, feeling the melancholy slowly vanish, "Well, things like how beautiful you are, your gentle nature, your ranch, your bank account."

Her face grew sober.

"Just kidding." I said, smiling wider.

She laughed, and the words that followed startled me.

"How many children should we have, Tobie?"

"Children?"

"Yes, children". She spoke. "You know, those things that crawl on the floor and wear diapers."

"And cry a lot." I told her. "Besides, don't you think marriage should be thought about before Children come along?"

I never had time to say anything else before her arms flew around me and she kissed me.

"Tobie," she said, bubbling, "I thought you'd never ask! Mr. Haskins, Ramirez, Spring," she shouted out excitedly. "Tobie has asked me to marry him". "And I've accepted."

I grinned as the three of them applauded and cheered, right there in the middle of a quiet peaceful Desert, beneath a night sky filled with a Million Brilliant Stars, a Full Moon casting its Golden Light, and two trusted friends any man could ask to have: all surrounding us in the shadow of one of the most remarkable Mountains on Earth… Granite Peak.

Putting my arm around Victoria, I pulled her close, "You know what?"

"What?" she asked.

"You, Victoria, can be very, very lovable…and exasperating."

With a wide smile, she kissed my cheek and whispered in my ear…" Yes. Isn't it exciting".